MIDNIGHT WITH THE DEVIL

EMMA CASTLE

EMMA CASTLE
Dark and Edgy Romance

PROLOGUE

WHAT TIME HIS PRIDE HAD CAST HIM OUT
FROM HEAVEN, WITH ALL HIS HOST OF REBEL
ANGELS. - JOHN MILTON, PARADISE LOST

"*How you have fallen from heaven, Morning Star, Son of the Dawn!*"

"*Favorite son no more!*"

"*No longer will you shine!*"

The taunts from his brother angels filled his head as he fell through the clouds. Light and darkness consumed him in flashing turns as he passed through the stars, into the clouds, and toward the earth. The air cut him, and the wind roared around him so deafening that his eardrums burst. Dawn was on the horizon, and he would die before he saw it fully claim the skies.

"*You, my brightest star, my favorite among the angels, how you have disappointed me.*" Father's voice was the hardest to bear.

Lucifer closed his eyes, welcoming the end, the death of light, the death of life.

"*You were to bring light into the world, inspire my creations, not corrupt them with your jealousies. Now you will rule the corrupted who follow you and become the king of hell.*"

The earth rose up to meet him, and he embraced the pain. His angelic heart shattered at the same moment his body broke upon impact. Everything went dark around him. Then bit by bit he became aware of himself, feeling every muscle, every bone, every atom that made up his body, screaming with pain. He hadn't died?

Lucifer gazed up at the endless clouds above him. The rift in the sky that would have let him back into the heavens was closed. He drew in a breath, the air like knives in his lungs. Something was different. He felt...empty. White feathers floated around him, their heavenly luminescence glinting in the sun.

My grace...it's gone.

It seemed like a millennium passed before he realized he lay upon the broken, cracked ground of the earth. His naked body hurt all over, but the pain was greatest along his shoulder blades. He was glad he could not see his back. There would be two terrible wounds replacing his snow-white wings. He reached out and grasped one of the remaining feathers that floated along the ground close to him and slipped it into the folds of the white tunic he wore. He needed that one bit of heaven, that one bit of *home*, or else he might go mad with grief.

The light inside him—the glowing essence that had once brought him only joy—was gone. There was nothing left inside him, nothing but darkness. He was in a crater in a desert land. Lucifer struggled to roll onto his stomach, his body too weak to stand.

He lifted his head, hearing the distant sounds of birds. Beyond the wasteland he'd fallen to, a beautiful Eden lay ahead, a land of green, full of beautiful beasts and flowers. Father had spoken so often about the world below the clouds.

Rage flooded through his body, giving him new energy and strength. Somewhere in that Eden were his father's favorite beings—*humans*. A vile word for vile beings who were no comparison to angels. But he was no longer an angel. He was fallen. A being without wings, without grace.

What am I now?

The question had no ready answer, and he cringed. For the first time in his existence, he didn't know what he really was.

He dug his hands into the arid dirt, clawing his way toward the garden ahead of him. At the center of the beautiful world, a single tree stood tall among the rest. Amidst its branches hung gleaming red apples. Father had spoken of this tree, the one that bore knowledge for the ages. Humans had free will, which angels did not, and if those humans dared break their promise to stay away from the tree, Lucifer would have his revenge and watch his father's favorite creations fall from grace.

Lucifer's lips twitched. He would not have long to wait to get his revenge. He could see the weakness and frailty in humanity. Bringing down the humans, one by one, would break his father's celestial heart, just as he had broken Lucifer's.

The wind carried away the feathers of his once angelic wings. He was glad he had caught one and tucked it safely near his heart. Paradise was lost to him, and he would make sure those damned humans would never reach it either.

I

BETTER TO REIGN IN HELL THAN SERVE IN
HEAVEN. - JOHN MILTON, PARADISE LOST

Hellfire Rising was a den of corruption.

A hotbed of sin and scandal.

Here hearts were broken, dreams destroyed, and dark fantasies realized.

It was the closest thing to a home Lucien Star had. He leaned against the balcony overlooking the dancers below, and with a snap of his fingers he held a glass of brandy. He took a slow sip, savoring the dark, hard flavor of the alcohol.

Two years ago, he had left behind the devil that his father expected him to be and remade himself into a different devil. Lucifer—the Morning Star, the once favored angel, the ruler of hell who never left the darkness—was gone. He was done spending the majority of his days in the dark abyss and the fires of hell in the realm of the evil and the damned. He stopped calling himself Lucifer and instead became Lucien Star. He used his powers to create a world that catered to his own desires, Hellfire Rising, a club in downtown Chicago.

He returned to the abyss, to the darkness, only when absolutely necessary to see to his duties. The gates of hell needed guarding, or else they would break and demons would flood into the world, destroying it. That was not what Lucien wanted. Contrary to popular opinion, he rather liked the human realm the way it was. He didn't want to see it destroyed by flames and left in eternal darkness.

A woman below him on the stairs glanced up, flashing him a sultry smile in open invitation. He raised his brandy glass in salute, but he wasn't interested. His mind was on other matters, the strange preoccupation with deep, troublesome thoughts so unlike him that it rattled the bars of the hellish emotional cage he felt trapped in tonight.

He wished hell could run itself, and it did...*mostly*. The damned didn't need him there to continue their suffering at all times, which was a relief. He despised hell. But he couldn't avoid his job completely. He had to watch out for stray demons that wandered into the paths of mortals, then catch and destroy them. That didn't give him joy either.

He preferred the mortal plane, watching humans make decisions that put them on the path to sin. He loved the secret language of hidden smiles, seductive glances, exploring hands as they gave themselves over to their darker desires. He craved corruption, not evil.

"Lucien." The smooth, dark voice caught Lucien's attention. He still stood at the edge of the balcony on the top floor of his club that led to his private office. From the relatively secluded spot, he could see the club patrons below him dancing wildly.

"Yes?" He turned away from the smoky haze of the strobe that lit the club below and faced Andras, one of his fellow fallen angels. The blond-haired man had the palest blue eyes, like frozen glaciers. They had once been brothers in the glittering city of clouds, but now they were brothers bound in darkness.

"You asked me to bring you a list of the deals made on

crossroads this month." Andras walked over to Lucien and held out his palm as though to shake his hand.

Lucien put his hand into Andras's, and his head suddenly filled with a flood of images. A hundred souls, a hundred deals made. Deals made out of anger, greed, and lust.

How utterly dull and predictable.

Lucien released Andras's hand and sighed as he turned back to face the crowd below. Andras joined him at the railing and remained quiet for a moment. Lucien again fixated on the feeling that had increasingly haunted him the last few years. He wasn't content. There was a cloying emptiness that seemed ready to strangle him, and he couldn't shake it. He was no stranger to that hollow feeling, but it seemed worse of late.

"Sir, you seem...unsatisfied."

Lucien nearly denied it, but he *never* lied. The devil only ever spoke the truth. Everyone painted him a liar, but it wasn't true. They lied to themselves and each other in his name.

"I am unsatisfied," he finally admitted. From the moment he'd been cast out of heaven, he had been restless and full of rage. The rage had faded over the many years he'd been in hell. Corrupting souls was too easy. A hint here, a little nudge there, and these mortals fell into sin so easily. He craved a challenge. The gates of hell required pure souls to be corrupted in order to stay strong. The more souls he took below, the stronger the powers keeping demons in hell were. In a strange way, corruption of a few protected millions. And it had been a long time since he'd focused on pure souls as targets. The gates were starting to crumble.

Nothing like a challenge when hell itself needed saving.

"Are there not any good, incorruptible souls still out there? The gates are weak. I can feel it," he muttered. It was a rhetorical question, but Andras straightened.

"There must be. Shall I find one for you? I too have been worried about the gates. It's been a long time since we've gone in search of pure souls to power the portal."

Lucien crossed his arms over his chest, frowning at the crowd below him. He hadn't expected Andras to offer to find one. He'd been thinking aloud more than anything, but Andras was a loyal soldier and clever. If anyone could find what he needed to protect the gates, it was Andras.

Do I want that? Would the challenge sate my emptiness? Or should I leave it up to Andras to secure the safety of hell?

No, he had to be the one to do it. When he corrupted the soul and secured it in hell, it kept the gates strong and the demons where they should be—locked away in crushing darkness.

If there was even the smallest chance of relieving himself of that awful ache, he had to try.

"Find me a pure soul. One that will be a true challenge. The gates need one that will truly test me if we are to secure the portal."

"Understood." Andras vanished, and the flutter of his invisible shadow wings was the only proof of his ever having been there. When Andras fell, he too had lost his snowy white wings. In their place, the scars had formed what were called shadow wings, and those were all that remained.

Lucien turned his back on the club and returned to his office. He closed the glass doors to his balcony and sat in his black leather desk chair. Taking a cigar from the cherrywood box, he removed his silver cigar cutter and cut the tip. Then he snapped his fingers, and a flame blossomed from his fingertips to light the cigar. He drew in a slow breath, relishing the rich, sweet aroma of the smoke, and blew the air back out. The smoke escaped his lips in tendrils that coiled into the air to form a slithering snake.

Andras would find him a soul, a perfect one to corrupt,

and it would restore Lucien's purpose and keep the gates of hell intact.

It's time the devil got back in the game.

LIFE ISN'T FAIR.

Diana Kingston knew that was the truth, but it didn't stop her from hoping for fairness every day. She sat by her father's hospital bed, helplessly watching him fight for life. He'd slipped into a coma early that morning as the final stages of cancer took hold. Her mother, Janet, held his hand and was talking softly to him about her day, hoping he could hear her. It had been a part of their normal routine before he'd slipped into the coma. When Diana got home from her college classes, she and her mother drove to the hospital to keep her father company while he went underwent radiation and chemotherapy for colon cancer. She couldn't get past the pain of watching her mother lose half of herself with the impending death of the man she had deeply loved for more than thirty years.

Most days Diana kept herself together, but today was possibly the end. The doctor had called her mother early this morning to say that her father, Hal, had slipped into a coma. Only yesterday, her father had been glassy-eyed and exhausted from fighting the inevitable but still awake and talking. The machines beeping beside his bed showed his life ticking away, slowly fading bit by bit. Her heart was breaking, fracturing like a mirror into a thousand shards. She could see herself in her father's face, reflected a thousand times over as he gave in to death inch by inch. Would her mother look at Diana and see that reflection of her father? Would it cause her mother even more pain? Diana bit her lip hard enough that the metallic taste of blood surprised her.

She licked her lip and rose from the stiff wooden hospital chair.

She was a coward, she was weak—she could not sit there and watch him die. It hurt too much.

"Mom, I'm going to get some air, okay?" She hugged her mother's shoulders and kissed her cheek before she headed to the door.

"Okay, hon," her mother murmured absently.

Diana paused at the door to her father's room, drinking in the sight of her parents. Hal was a handsome man with soft gray eyes, eyes that would likely never open again, and brown hair feathered with gray. Her mother, Janet, had been a real beauty in her youth and was still stunning with gray-blue eyes and raven hair. But her father's illness had aged them both over the last two year, stealing time like fall leaves scattered upon the wind.

When her father died, the blow would crush her mother. They were soul mates. Diana had grown up in a house filled with life and laughter, songs sung in the sun, and dancing in the moonlight. Her parents had a peaceful life, but now life seemed determined to claw back some of the perfection it had given away too freely.

Tears welled up in Diana's eyes as she stepped into the hallway of the oncology wing at Saint Francis Hospital outside Chicago.

Just breathe, she reminded herself. She wiped her eyes, smearing the tears across her cheeks. She been raised Catholic, but her faith had never been that strong, not until her father fell ill. Now she prayed like the world was ending, because for her, part of it was.

"You okay?" A nurse came over and gently touched her shoulder in the nice way people do to strangers in pain.

"Yeah," she whispered. "Just a bad day for my dad." The

words "he's dying" couldn't come out. She didn't want—and frankly couldn't handle—anyone's pity right now.

The woman nodded in immediate understanding. "Everyone has those bad days here, but they're usually followed by good ones. Hang in there, sweetie." The nurse's brown eyes were tender as she smiled.

"Thanks." Diana tucked a lock of hair behind her ear and glanced around, wishing she could get outside fast, but the hospital was a labyrinth of wings, elevator bays, and nurses' stations.

"Why don't you take a break in the chapel?" The nurse's suggestion sounded good.

Diana thanked her again and walked toward the end of the hall. She reached it and glanced at the door with a little plaque that said "Healing Chapel." As she entered, she held her breath, but the chapel was empty. A stained-glass window of Saint Francis of Assisi standing in the woods surrounded by animals was at the back of the chapel. She'd come here often these last few weeks, and while she was a lapsed Catholic, she knew enough of the saints to know Assisi. He'd become a quiet comfort to her.

The pews gleamed with a splash of colorful light pouring in from the stained glass. Diana walked to the first row and sat down, then closed her eyes as more tears trailed down her cheeks. Two years ago all that had mattered in her life was college. She would be a senior at the University of Chicago this fall, majoring in architecture. When her dad fell ill, her mother had done her best to hide it from her.

Part of Diana was angry that her dad was ill, angry that he was putting her and her mother through hell. And she was angry that she wouldn't be able to fix her mother's broken heart. She was angry most of all at herself for not being able to do a damn thing to help him. Anger felt good, and it made her feel strong, even if only for a short time.

She wasn't sure how long she sat there before she realized she wasn't alone. The fine hair at the back of her neck rose as she had that eerie sensation of unseen eyes gazing upon her. Some ancient instinct warned her that she was in the presence of a predator.

Turning slowly, she looked over her shoulder, near the dimly lit entry. She saw a figure that was wreathed in shadows. For a second, she couldn't breathe. It was as if every nightmare she'd ever had about shapes in the dark, choking, suffocating, and endless nothingness buried in layers of smoke were all there in that doorway. Then she blinked and the shadows vanished.

Instead, a man stood framed in the doorway. His black suit and red silk tie were strangely intense for a hospital setting. She was so used to seeing people in casual, comfortable clothes while they spent long hours at the bedside of a loved one. He held himself in a confident, dominant manner that made her shiver. Gazing upward, she gulped when she realized he was staring at her with the same intensity. The instant their eyes locked, her breath rushed out of her and all the thoughts in her head rattled around. Those eyes—fathomless twin pools of deadly intent that she couldn't understand—caused fear to sink its claws into her as every basic animal instinct in her shrieked to run. She blinked and the strange, frightening spell was somewhat broken, and she was able to take in the rest of his face.

He was frighteningly attractive, like a model from a fashion magazine. He had dark hair, not quite black, and his eyes were just as dark. She could see no hint of warmth there. His features were perfect, a straight nose, chiseled jaw, and full lips that a girl could get lost in daydreams about kissing. There was an edge of danger about him, something that warned her deep down to be careful, to not run, because she was prey and he was a predator. As silly as the thought was, she sensed it was true on some level. She had to be careful.

Yet Diana couldn't help but wonder about this man and who he might be. He was fascinating to look at. She had dated her fair share of guys, but this man...he made the whole world fall away. He was completely absorbing in a way she couldn't explain.

Silence stretched between them. She wanted to wipe away the tears drying on her cheeks, but she couldn't move, frozen by both fear and enchantment.

"I hope I didn't disturb your prayers."

She shivered at his low, silken voice. That voice could tempt a woman to think of her darkest fantasies. Fantasies she fought every day to ignore, yet she couldn't stop her body's reaction. She pulled her control together and forced herself to finally move. She had to get out of this room. Her instincts still screamed at her to get the hell out of there.

"Er...no, I was just leaving." She stood and exited the pew.

He took a step closer, sliding his hands into the pockets of his black pants. The light from the windows moved over him in the strangest way, as though he was bending the light to move away from him, leaving him more in shadow.

Was that even possible? Diana glanced around, very aware that she was alone with this man, and the cold, emotionless faces of the occupants of the stained-glass windows weren't there to help her.

"Visiting someone?"

"My...dad." Just saying it dispelled the fear and desire that this man created inside her. She wiped at her eyes, making sure he couldn't see any fresh tears.

"I'm sorry." He took another step closer, his gaze sliding from her to the stained-glass window behind her. He stared at Saint Francis with an odd, knowing smile as if he were intimately familiar with the saint, which of course wasn't possible.

"Thank you." She grappled for something polite to say. "Are you visiting someone here too?" She studied his profile and the way the light from the stained glass fractured over his features in dozens of colors.

His lips curled in a ghost of a grin. "Not exactly."

"Are you a doctor?" If he wasn't there visiting, he had to be there for some reason, right?

He suddenly chuckled as if at some private joke. "Do I look like I save lives?"

"I...I'm sorry, I just assumed." She started for the door again, disturbed and way too interested in the man.

"Diana, wait."

Her name upon his lips stopped her dead in her tracks.

"How do you know who I am?" Terror clenched her throat so hard the words barely escape her mouth.

The man turned to face her. His head inclined toward her, his body moving with a slow grace, his eyes pinning her in place as he came closer.

"You sent a prayer out for your father."

Stunned, she nodded.

"I'm here to answer your prayer."

His dark eyes seem to swallow her whole as his words punched her gut. Was this some kind of cruel joke? Was he a doctor playing a game? Or worse, just some creep who lurked in hospital chapels to prey on emotional women?

"I'm not a creep lurking around waiting to prey on emotional women."

He chuckled again, the darkness edging the sound giving her chills. He'd heard her thoughts. "But...how? You're not a doctor. You said you don't save lives. I don't understand—"

He raised one hand, index finger pointing up to command silence. She closed her mouth. The man drifted closer step by step, and she still couldn't move. They were now only a foot apart, and she could feel that awful, crushing darkness rolling off him in waves.

"I'm not a doctor, and I only save lives when there's something in it for me."

Diana wrapped her arms around herself. "I still don't understand."

"Of course you don't. You're a sweet, innocent mortal. No need to worry. I am happy to spell it out for you." He reached out to touch her cheek.

Suddenly the chapel vanished around them and they were in front of her father's room, peering in at him and her mother from the doorway. Her father lay still, his face waxen with approaching death, and the sight tore at her heart so fiercely she nearly cried out. The man from the chapel was right behind her, his warm breath fanning against her neck. She shivered.

"I make life-changing *deals*."

"Deals?" She didn't understand how they'd gotten from the chapel to her father's room.

I'm dreaming. That has to be it. No one around them moved. The nurses at the station were frozen, her parents too. The multiple monitors connected to her father were still and silent. This was how all her nightmares went. She couldn't move, couldn't scream, she just had to face whatever was happening. This was most definitely a dream.

"Yes." The man's voice was low, seductive, like a lover. "You want your father to be well again, don't you?"

"Of course I do." Diana stared at her father, his face a mask of pain and exhaustion.

"What would you give for him to be healed?"

She spun to face the dark-eyed man and came face-to-face with his red necktie. He was towering over her; he had to be at least six feet three. She barely came up to his shoulders.

"I..."

"Think now, think hard." The man's dark eyes lowered to her lips as though he was thinking about kissing her. A wild flush rippled through her.

"I would give anything."

"*Anything* is an awfully dangerous word." His dark eyes were like fathomless pools, but in them she saw her father walking, laughing, alive. The hunger for that moment, to see her father healthy and happy, was so strong that she was able to shed her fears of this man and bravely speak the truth.

She pursed her lips for a minute but then nodded. "Anything."

He studied her, and she refused to flinch beneath his assessing gaze. She straightened her back and lifted her chin, wanting to project confidence. The man seemed amused by her sudden change, and a slow, seductive smile lifted the corners of his lips.

"Would you give yourself to *me*? Sell your soul?" the man asked, his voice hard-edged beneath that layer of silken seduction.

"Sell my..."

"Soul." He opened his palm, holding it flat as though waiting for her to take his hand.

"What do you mean, my soul?"

"I'll show you." He extended his hand closer to hers. She reached out, hesitating, but then finally placed her hand in his. The second his fingers curled around hers she was swallowed by darkness.

Fluttering sounds like the rush of a raven's wings in the night made her shiver, and she clung to his hand, which still grasped hers. All around her was nothingness, and she couldn't seem to get any air into her lungs for a long second. Then finally she was able to speak.

"What is this?" she whispered, fear choking her.

"The end of everything you know and love."

"Hell," she breathed. Where were the fires and the evil souls?

"Hell is different for everyone. It's not all fire and brimstone." His chuckle curled around her, hot and seductive.

"I see only darkness," she gasped.

"Because your hell is one of *nothingness*."

Suddenly they were back in the chapel, and Diana fell to her knees, shaking violently. He stood above her, hands tucked in his trouser pockets, waiting patiently.

"You agree to make a deal with me, and I will give you something in return."

She put a hand to her chest as she looked up at him.

"You can...save my dad?" Part of her wondered if she was dreaming. She had to be. There was no way she was talking to the devil about making a deal to save her father's life.

"I can."

"But you said you don't save lives."

The man—no, the devil—slowly smiled. "I said I don't *look* like I save lives, and as a general rule I do not."

"Then why help me?" Diana got to her feet but sat down on the nearest pew. The devil strode to the stained-glass window, tilting his face up, the light playing upon his skin.

"Because you are a pure soul and I hunger for corruption. I need to *corrupt* you."

"Corrupt me?" She shuddered at the dark word. When she thought of corruption, she thought of stealing, of hurting people, of unlawful things she'd never do.

The devil turned to face her again, and the shadows pooled around him, his eyes suddenly glowing with a soft ruby-red gleam.

"I want to own your body, your soul, to show you the pleasures of the dark side. I want you to tell me every wicked fantasy, the worst ones, and I want you to let me act them out with you. When I claim a pure soul through pleasure and bring it to the darkness, that soul then belongs to me in every way."

Her darkest fantasies? She struggled to think, but she didn't have any fantasies.

"*Everyone* has fantasies, Diana. Even pure souls like you."

"You...you said you make deals, right? What would our deal be?" She couldn't believe she was considering this, but if it meant saving her father, how could she not listen to what the devil offered? He would own her soul. Was her father's life worth letting him drag her down into eternal darkness?

"You will come to me every Friday night at midnight. I can do with you as I please until dawn, then you can leave."

"For how long?" She tried not to think about what the devil would do with her.

"Three months. It will be a delightful gift to myself to celebrate the anniversary of my fall from grace. When you die, whenever that may be, your soul will be fully mine, trapped forever in that nothingness I showed you."

Twelve Fridays? She could survive whatever the devil wanted for her father's sake. She wouldn't think about what would happen when she died someday and how she'd be trapped—in hell—with him. "How...how do I know you won't let him die after you're through with me?"

The devil's grin was scary, not because *he* was scary but because that sexy grin promised all sorts of sins, ones she didn't think she could handle. "I may be the devil, but I'm not a liar. I get what I, and I promise on my black heart you'll get what you want."

She didn't immediately respond. Diana wasn't stupid. She'd seen movies about deals with the devil. There was always a catch, and the trick was finding out what it was.

"What about my mom, or any other friends or family?

You'll save my dad but let someone else that I love die instead, right?"

His eyes widened the slightest bit, and then he smiled as though pleased she wasn't simply agreeing.

"That is called cosmic balance, you clever child, and no, I do not have to bend to the will of cosmic balance. You won't face anyone else's death because of our little deal."

Diana couldn't ignore the possessiveness that seemed to emanate from him as he gazed at her. Was her soul really worth it to him? If so, then she had one heck of a bargaining chip, and she refused to waste it.

"I want you to promise that *no one* I love gets hurt and my dad gets totally healed forever."

He waved a finger at her. "Now, now, you can't demand—"

"Do you want my pure soul or not?" The second she issued her challenge, invisible electricity sparked between them. The heat burning through Diana held a promise of what was to come, and it scared the hell out of her. She had to make this deal, but only on *her* terms. If he didn't agree, she still had the power to walk away, and she would.

When he didn't respond, she stood up and started toward the chapel door.

"Fine." He growled the word as he came up behind her. She turned to look at him, stepping back instinctively as he came too close. "I can give your other loved ones extra protection, but if the other side makes a decision, that's on your precious angels, not me. I don't have control over what those winged idiots do. But I swear that nothing I do will cause them harm."

"Okay, so three months of my submitting to you and you heal my dad."

"Submitting?" He laughed. "That's a rather interesting word. Is that one of your fantasies? To have me dominating you?"

Diana shuddered at first, but then an inner voice whispered, *"Yes. Dominate me."* A voice she'd buried every time the desires surfaced, because it filled her with shame "Is that the deal?" she repeated.

The devil grinned. "Yes. That's the deal."

"Do we...shake on it or something?" She held out her hand. He eyed it and then took her hand in his and tugged. She fell against him, surprised at the feel of his warm body against hers.

Before she could push him away, he bent his head and whispered, "You *always* seal a devil's bargain with a kiss." And then he slanted his mouth over hers, burning her lips with his as he ravaged her mouth, his tongue seeking hers. She was too stunned at first, but as his mouth softened on hers, she melted into him.

A frightening sense of falling forever in the darkness and fluttering black wings surged through her, but he held her, banding his arms around her and tethering her so she wouldn't vanish in the nothingness.

She tried to banish her fears, praying for one spot of light in the darkness as they kissed. There was a brilliant flash of bright light, the feel of soft downy feathers brushing against her cheek, and then she glimpsed a shining city in the clouds.

Then it was gone. The nothingness remained.

His lips left hers, and the warmth of his body faded. Dimly, she heard his silken whisper in her mind. *"You are mine now, Diana."*

When she opened her eyes and jolted awake, she lay on one of the pews in the hospital's chapel.

She'd only had a wild dream. Her father wouldn't get better. A tear rolled off her cheek onto the fabric of the seat beneath her. She sat up slowly, combed her fingers through her hair, and tried to compose herself. Then she left the chapel and returned to her father's room. As the door to the chapel closed behind her, she swore she heard a faint, low masculine chuckle.

"I'm going crazy. The stress of all this is getting to me."

As much as she would've done anything to save her dad, there was no such thing as bargaining with the devil. Because she didn't believe in the devil.

BUT HIS DOOM RESERVED HIM TO MORE
WRATH; FOR NOW THE THOUGHT BOTH OF
LOST HAPPINESS AND LASTING PAIN
TORMENTS HIM. - JOHN MILTON, PARADISE
LOST

L ucien stood in the chapel, invisible to Diana, watching her wipe away her tears and leave the room. She was a beautiful woman, with dark-brown hair and dove-gray eyes that reminded him of lightning in winter snowstorms. He'd seen lovelier women, yet there was something about her that drew him in, a natural beauty that seemed to come from within. It was possible that her pure soul was calling to him, but the longing to thread his hands through the straight waterfall of her hair...that was pure lust on his part.

"You don't believe in me yet, but you will." And by the time she realized what bargain she'd made, it would be too late. Her soul would be forever trapped in his clutches, corrupted by his darkness, and that soul would keep the gates of hell strong and secure.

After she left, he raised a hand to his lips, brushing the tips of his fingers over them, wondering.

It had been a most curious thing. When he'd kissed her and sealed their bargain, he had thought he'd seen something, just a quick second of a young girl's hand brushing over cool blades of grass on a summer morning, the chilly drops of dew tickling his fingers as they tickled hers. It had felt...*heavenly*. He'd convinced himself that he didn't want to remember what heaven felt like, how it tasted, how it looked, but kissing Diana had brought back forbidden memories. He buried the rush of pleasure that thoughts of heaven brought because it always brought back the pain of his fall. Instead, he focused on why he would experience that with Diana when he never had with any other mortal before.

He normally saw people's darkest desires when he sealed their bargains. He exited the chapel and moved unseen through the hospital until he reached the room where Diana and her mother were saying their goodbyes for the night and going home. After they had left, he walked over to where Diana's father lay breathing softly, his eyes closed. Lucien stared down at him for a long minute. The man was deep in a coma, wouldn't last the night, not that Diana or her mother knew that. They only knew that time was limited. The doctors had assured them they would have another day or two to say goodbye and take him off the machines. But even the machines couldn't stop the death that was creeping through Hal's body.

Lucien reached out and woke Hal from the coma. Diana's father's eyes slowly opened up, and he had the look of a man lost, a man who'd begun his travel to the other side but had been pulled abruptly back.

"You've come for me?" The man opened his eyes, and they were soft gray eyes just like Diana's.

"I'm not Death. He's the one who pays house calls," Lucien said with a sardonic smile.

"This isn't a house call?" Hal coughed and winced, and then he relaxed, his eyes starting to close as he struggled to stay awake.

Lucien watched all this in fascination, strangely reminded

of his own fall and the struggle to go on. The human will to survive, to overcome any obstacle, even one as painful as death, was so strong.

"So if you aren't Death, and there's no way you're a doctor, then who are you?" Hal asked. Pain filled his voice, but he sounded strong now too. Lucien felt a stab of pride in knowing a man like this had fathered his newest pet, for that was what Diana would be: his pet, a plaything, one he would take good care of even while corrupting her with her own forbidden desires.

"I don't think you want to know who I am." Lucien picked up the charts at the end of hospital bed, flicking through the complicated pages.

"Try me," Hal challenged.

Lucien put his charts down and walked around the side of the bed, offering a hand. Hal placed his hand in Lucien's just like Diana had, and he showed Hal exactly who he was by letting Hal glimpse his own personal hell just as he had shown Diana hers.

Hal's face paled even more. "You're the...the..."

"Yes." Lucien didn't bother to say the word. He'd never been overly fond of *devil* or *Satan*. They were such negative words for a being who'd once been named heaven's brightest star.

"That's not...you can't be..." Diana's father struggled to accept the truth, but after a long moment, he seemed too tired to fight.

"I am. You'd better believe it," Lucien replied.

"But why are you here?" Hal asked, eyes wide. "I've tried to be a good man."

"And...luckily, you succeeded."

"I don't understand."

"I'm not dragging you down to hell. Scout's honor." Lucien chuckled, but Hal didn't laugh.

"I'm here because your daughter just bought you the winning lottery ticket."

"What are you talking about?" Hal blinked in shock as Lucien placed a palm on his forehead.

"Don't worry, you won't remember any of this."

Hal's eyes closed, and white light went from Lucien's hand into Hal's head. The last vestiges of his angelic powers—oddly the ones the heavens hadn't taken from him when they'd taken almost everything else—still worked.

Lucien dropped his hand from Hal's face and glanced toward the machine that now beeped in a steady rhythm.

Come dawn, the doctors would be baffled by Hal's quick recovery, and they would send him home, declaring it a miracle.

But for Diana it was to be a debt. A debt he was very interested in collecting. There was a momentary flicker of guilt at knowing he would be Diana's destruction, but he buried it deep inside. The devil couldn't afford to feel guilty, not when the universe's very stability relied on him remaining a selfish bastard and stealing pure souls. For Diana it would it would mean surrendering her pure soul to the realm of darkness so that her soul could fortify the gates and keep all hell from literally breaking loose.

☙❧

DIANA SLEPT IN, NOT WANTING TO LEAVE THE COMFORT OF her warm bed in her little apartment. If she was being honest, she didn't want to face today. She and her mother had spoken to the doctor, and today they would take him off the machines keeping him alive. The doctor wasn't certain how long it would take for her father to die, but Diana knew it could be a few days. He was so damn strong, had always been strong, and he would cling to life while she and her mother watched in agony.

I can't face that, not yet.

Outside the sun was up, light peeking in through the pale-blue curtains on her bedroom window. For a long moment she lay there, thinking about the frightening dream she'd had when she'd fallen asleep in the chapel the day before.

A deal with the devil.

She sighed heavily and forced herself out of bed. Diana couldn't put off the visit to the hospital any longer. Her mother would need her there, and it would be one of the last times she would get to see her father before...before he was gone. She trembled, and a chill stole through her, settling deep into her bones. Whenever she thought of her dad being gone, it left a burning, hollow ache inside her chest. It would only get worse once he was really gone.

She picked up her cell phone from her nightstand and checked the time. It was nearly noon on a Sunday morning. She'd missed several calls from her mother. Heart pounding, she called her mom back. Something had happened to her dad before she'd had a chance to say goodbye? She tried not to think about it, about how pale he had been last night.

"Diana! Thank God!" her mother gasped when she answered the phone.

"What is it? Dad?" Diana's voice broke, and she was seconds away from crying.

"Yes, but I think it's good news. He came out of the coma. I think..." Her mother choked on a sob. "I think he might be in remission."

"What?" Diana wiped the fresh stream of tears on her cheeks. She didn't understand.

"It's a miracle! Your father called me at around nine. He woke up at six this morning feeling better than he's been in a long time.

He called the nurses to have the doctors come see him. They ran some tests and biopsied his colon." Her mother took a deep breath before continuing. "They didn't find any cancer cells."

That couldn't be possible. Yesterday he had been mere days away from death.

"Mom, they made a mistake," Diana said. "They had to."

"They tested him several times on several different machines to be sure."

Diana bit her lip so hard she tasted blood. It was too dangerous to let hope take over. Far too dangerous.

"So what does this mean?" she asked her mother.

"I think he can come home in a few days. I'm headed to the hospital now."

"I can meet you there."

"No, no," her mother said. "Let me go. Just in case." The words she left unsaid were loud in the silence between them. In case it really was a mistake. Better to have only her mother's hopes broken than both of them. But Diana didn't want her facing that news alone.

"I'm coming." Diana hung up on her mother before she could protest, and she hastily dressed and grabbed her keys. Her orange tabby cat, Seth, was perched on the arm of the couch in the small living room, purring as she walked by.

"I'll be back later," she told the cat. He lowered onto his stomach and tucked his paws under his chest, watching her as she slung her purse over her shoulder and slipped outside.

By the time she reached the hospital, she was a nervous wreck. Her hands wouldn't stop shaking. She parked her car and headed toward the oncology department, but when she got to the hall leading to her father's room, the hairs on the back of her neck rose and she had that eerie sensation of someone watching her.

Just like in my dream.

Diana glanced about but didn't see anyone except for the nurses at their stations.

"We made a deal. Don't forget it." The soft, seductive voice slithered inside her mind, and she froze a step away from the door to her father's room.

No. It had been a dream. Their encounter hadn't been real. The man, the devil, that kiss—it had all been a dream.

"You promised me your soul, and I will collect."

Diana shook her head, trying to banish the voice, and she rushed into her father's room.

Hal sat in bed, his face full of color and smiling. Her mother spoke to a doctor who was showing her some lab results. It all seemed so surreal. Last night he'd been still and pale as death, his hands clammy to the touch and his chest barely moving with shallow breaths. The man in the hospital before her now was healthy and bright-eyed. Her heart stung with an overwhelming rush of joy.

"Hey." Diana greeted her father and kissed him and hugged him. He returned her hug, and she was startled by the strength of his embrace. The last few months he had been too weak to do anything but squeeze her hand.

"Hey, kiddo. I think I might be going home in a few days. Can you believe it?" Her father's eyes sparkled with life in a way she couldn't remember. He had been ill for two years now, and she had started to forget the man he had been before the cancer.

"Yeah, Mom called me. I can't believe it." She hugged him again, her heart clenching in her chest.

"It could be that the treatments really worked and we are just now finally seeing the results," the doctor explained. "Either way, I think this is good, Mrs. Kingston. We'll continue to run tests for a few more days to be sure, but I'd like to plan on sending him home on Wednesday."

Her mother beamed at the doctor. "Wednesday?"

"Yes." The doctor smiled. "I try not to let patients get their hopes up, but in this case, things look very good."

"Thank you." Her mother hugged the startled physician and then returned to her husband's bedside.

"I'll leave you all to have some time with him, but make sure he has plenty of rest."

Diana pulled up a chair by her father's hospital bed and grasped one of his hands between hers, squeezing it gently.

She stayed at the hospital for two more hours, her mind reeling as her father got up on shaky legs for the first time in weeks. She didn't understand how this was the same man from the day before—the man who had lain on the bed, so close to death that it hung around him like a shroud. Could her strange dream have been real? Was she actually considering that she'd made an actual honest-to-God deal with the devil? She turned on her laptop and googled "deals with the devil" first thing after she arrived home. As the search history revealed information, she held her breath and read on.

She found several articles about the mythology behind making a deal with the devil. There were even descriptions of rituals for summoning a demon at a crossroads to make the bargain. Seth perched on the edge of her desk, his face alert on the front door, his tail flicking back and forth.

"It's Sunday. No mail today," she reminded the tabby and stroked a hand down his spine. He arched, encouraging her to scratch his lower back right above his tail. Suddenly the mail slot on her door opened, and a letter dropped onto the floor.

Diana stared at the letter. She hadn't heard anyone come up the stairs. She always heard steps on the stairs.

Seth's ears flattened, and he let out an eerie meow. He only made that noise when she vacuumed too close to him under the bed.

Unease prickled along her skin like thousands of invisible spiders, making her shudder. She set her laptop aside and approached the letter cautiously. It was made of expensive crisp white card stock and bound with a red satin ribbon. She picked it up off the carpet and turned it over. There was no return address, only her name, *Diana Kingston*, scrawled on top in flowing cursive.

Diana tugged on the ribbon until the bow fell apart, and then she unfolded the letter to read it.

Ms. Kingston,

You have recently completed a transaction with His Majesty, the king of hell. You are hereby to give yourself over to his desires for three months in exchange for your father's life. You will be ready each Friday night at half past eleven. A black sedan will pick you up. He will bring you to a place where you will fulfill your obligations. If at any point you wish to rescind this contract by invoking the free will clause specified in the attached contract article 2 section 1, then you must face the immediate death of your father.

Any questions regarding your contract with Lucien Star, a.k.a. Lucifer Morningstar, a.k.a. the devil, can be written and directed to Mr. Star's counsel, Lionel Barnaby, Esq.

Sincerely,

Mr. Barnaby

Diana read the letter over several times, unsure whether she wanted to laugh or cry. "I really made a deal with the devil?"

Something brushed against her leg and she jumped, her heart jolting into her throat as she almost screamed. Seth hissed and bounded away from her, upset that he had scared her enough that she jumped.

"Jesus, Seth." She stared at the vanishing tail of her cat as he whipped around the corner and into her bedroom.

She glanced back down at the letter and then turned the page to see a few more pages of intense-looking legal terms. "Terms and conditions." She scanned the frighteningly long list that made very little sense to her. But she searched for the clause about free will.

"In accordance with the ruling laws of heaven and hell, a human shall *always* have free will, even during transactions with the devil. Any sale of the soul, permanently or temporarily, to the devil to receive benefits is valid and binding unless the mortal exclaims, 'I invoke my right of free will.' At such point the transaction is broken, and the benefit conferred upon the mortal will be undone or taken away."

Diana stared at the contract and read the signature lines at the bottom where her name had been written in her own hand. She brushed her fingertips over the signature to feel the ink, and the memory of kissing the devil flooded back. The heat, the sensual dominance, the feel of wind whipping around her all swept through her like a roaring wave. Gasping, she struggled for air. She'd sealed her deal with a kiss. In some of the crossroads mythology articles she'd read, that was how bargains were made.

It is real.

She set the contract and the letter down on her desk, returned to her couch, and picked up her laptop once more. She had no idea what she was looking for. Answers, maybe? But even the internet was no help. She searched for books about the devil and the occult, and a psychic bookshop popped up in the search results. She clicked on the address and saw that it was only two miles away and was open until ten.

Diana cast a look at Seth. He lay on his back in the middle of the floor, his tail twitching.

"Should I go?" she asked. Seth's tail stilled. "Is that a yes?" she confirmed, half smiling as Seth rolled onto his side and looked up at her.

"Fine. I'll go." She closed her laptop and fetched her purse. She exited the apartment and typed the bookstore's address into her phone. By the time she reached the bookstore, the sun hung heavy in the sky. Diana parked her car and faced the shop.

A small sign dangled off the metal pole above the door. Its painted black lettering stood out against the pale gray background: *The Occultist's Apothecary*. The shop was surrounded by a coffee shop on one side and a consignment clothing store on the other side. Only the coffee shop was open, but it had few customers.

Diana adjusted her purse on her shoulder and headed toward the bookstore. A small bell tinkled above her head as she entered. The musty smell of old books, candles, incense, and spices filled the air like an invisible cloud.

There was part of the shop that had a counter with bottles and other ingredients. A beautiful dark-skinned woman stood behind the counter, sorting out receipts. She flicked her gaze up and then back to her task.

"Excuse me," Diana said uncertainly. "I'm looking for some books."

God, she's going to think I'm crazy.

"Books about what?" The woman's voice was soft and deep, lovely. Her dark eyes lifted again and held on Diana's face. Her expression was unreadable.

"Um..." Diana had to stop herself from glancing around. "The devil. Specifically about making deals...like at a crossroads."

"Crossroads deal," the woman said slowly, her gaze sharpening.

"Yes, or something like that," Diana added. She and the devil hadn't really been at a crossroads. Or had they? The hospital was at an intersection of two streets. Maybe that qualified?

"You making deals with the dark one, child?" the woman asked.

"I'm twenty-one." She wasn't a kid.

The woman's lips twitched. "What's your name?"

"Diana."

"The Huntress, a goddess's name. It's good to have a strong name of the old gods." The woman held out her hand over the counter. Diana reached out to shake it, but the woman caught her hand and turned Diana's palm face up, peering closely at it. Then she ran a fingertip along her skin, tracing lines.

"You..." The woman's brow furrowed, and she held out her other hand. She examined both of Diana's palms, frowning.

"What's wrong?" Diana peered down at her own hand.

"A person's palm should have heart and lifelines that are similar but not exact. Yours...match."

Diana had never really thought about her palms, but she did know the lines didn't match. Yet as she looked at her hands now, they were exactly the same.

"Oh, child, what have you done?" the woman demanded in a soft, breathless voice, her brown eyes heavy with worry.

"What do you mean?"

"Come and sit." The woman motioned for Diana to follow her back behind a black curtain. She hesitated a second before following. There was a small table covered with a dark-purple cloth and a tea tray. The woman poured two cups of tea and handed Diana one.

"Drink it all." The woman waited while Diana drained the small cup of tea. The woman took the cup and overturned it on its saucer for a moment, then turned it back over. She peered into the bottom of the teacup and frowned.

"You wanted to save your father?"

"Yes." Diana stared at the woman. *How could she know?*

"The dark one came to you and made a deal for your father's life?"

Again, Diana nodded and whispered, "Yes."

"You gave him your body, not just your soul." The woman pursed her lips, turning the cup a little. "He's going to break you, child. No one ever survives a deal like that."

"Break me?" Diana wrapped her arms around her chest, a chill slithering down her spine.

"You are not the first woman to catch his eye. He loves pleasure in all forms."

The woman set the cup down and gently touched Diana's shoulders.

"Is there anything I can do?" Diana asked. She wouldn't rescind the contract because her father's life was at risk, but if there was anything she could do to protect herself, she would.

"Come with me." The woman escorted her back to the front of the store, and she retrieved a small box behind the counter. She sat down and opened it.

A small wooden cross on a leather cord sat inside the box.

"This is a talisman that has been blessed by a saint. Take it. Though I do not know what good it will do."

"I thought crosses only worked on vampires?"

The woman laughed. "Child, crosses do not work on vampires. Vampires are not demons."

Diana blinked. "Are you saying vampires are real?"

"You made a deal with the devil, and you don't believe in vampires?" The woman laughed softly. "Child, the dark is full of monsters, human and other."

"Vampires..." She didn't know what to say. Her world, or what she knew of it, was vanishing overnight. She slipped the cross over her neck and tucked it beneath her sweater.

"How much do I owe you for the reading and the cross?"

The woman held out a hand. "Nothing. My name is Amara. You may come back anytime you need me."

"Really?" Diana wanted to hug Amara and did so, ignoring the woman's outstretched hand. Amara patted her back before they broke apart, but her eyes were serious as she looked at Diana.

"You must be careful. The more you surrender to the dark, to him, the more you will lose yourself. You must find the light inside you and hold on to it. Do not go into his darkness—it will destroy you."

"Thank you." Diana touched the cross hidden beneath her sweater and waved goodbye to Amara before she exited the shop.

A bitter wind curled around her, icy fingers teasing her hair and digging into her clothes, making her shiver. She rushed to her car and got inside. She turned on the lights and thought—for just one second only—that someone was in the back seat. She spun, gasping, but the back seat was empty. She turned back to the steering wheel, her heart pounding and her blood roaring in her ears. She would have sworn there'd been a flash of light, like the yellow of an animal's eyes in the rearview mirror.

"I'm going crazy. I just need to go home and rest."

"Rest." A deep voice laughed in the back of her mind. *"You'll need it."*

Diana closed her eyes, breathing in slowly.

Stay calm. You have to stay rational. I will face this devil and the deal and save my dad. I won't let him break me.

When she opened her eyes again she felt better, more clearheaded, until she heard the voice one last time.

"I will have you in every way I desire."

❧ 3 ❧

CHAINED ON THE BURNING LAKE, NOR EVEN
THENCE HAD RISEN OR HEAVED HIS HEAD,
BUT THAT THE WILL AND HIGH PERMISSION
OF ALL-RULING HEAVEN LEFT HIM AT LARGE
TO HIS OWN DARK DESIGNS. - JOHN MILTON,
PARADISE LOST

Amara Dimka locked the door to her shop and flipped the Open sign to Closed. After reading that poor girl's palm and tea leaves, she didn't want to face any more customers. She needed to recover from the rush of premonitions. Touching the other side always took a toll on her. She'd caught a glimpse of a shining city, heard a flutter of wings in the dark, and then her stomach had dropped to her feet as she'd sensed the *end*. The end of everything. Amara paused and leaned against the counter for a minute, catching her breath.

That young woman was in danger, but there was no way to help her. One did not simply defy the dark one.

She put a few books back on the shelves, then fetched a broom from the storage closet and made a quick pass through the shop, collecting a small amount of dust. She leaned the broom against the counter and bent to retrieve a dustpan on a shelf away from where customers could see it. She gripped the handle and froze. *Something* was in her shop.

A chill trickled down her spine, and she suppressed a shiver. She stood slowly, and it took every ounce of her self-control not to flinch when she found herself face-to-face with one of the most beautiful men she'd ever seen. He wore a tailored black suit and a red tie. His dark hair was a little long, and it gleamed as if lit by sunlight although the sun had already set. His eyes were obsidian and eerily unreadable of any emotion.

"Can I help you?" she asked carefully. There was no doubt who this man was.

"I think you can, Amara." His voice was silky and low, like a lover's voice.

She waited, her heart racing.

"You can stay out of my business." His dark eyes flashed with red fire.

"With the girl, Diana?" Amara's heartbeat felt heavy in her chest because she knew her words might sound like a challenge. She didn't want to bow down to him. She was a white witch, not one who followed him. She believed in helping people.

"Yes." The dark one trailed a finger along the counter as though checking for dust, but his finger left a burning path on the counter with a charred black line in the wood.

"I don't hear about *you* making any deals these days." She couldn't help but wonder what had changed for him that he would make this deal personally. "People usually visit me after signing up with a crossroads demon. What's so special about this one that you did the deal yourself?" Amara tried to act casual, as though she wasn't having a conversation with the king of hell. She bent down to retrieve the dustpan and picked up her broom. Then she finished sweeping up the dirt and dust bunnies.

The devil followed behind her, pausing at a shelf of books on witchcraft and plucking a title off to flip idly through the pages.

"She's...pure," he finally said.

"Nobody is pure," Amara replied without thinking.

"I don't mean pure as in free of sin. Everyone makes that mistake." He paused in the study of a book on the Salem witch trials and smirked. Then he waved the book at her. "Poor women, white witches, not dark ones, yet they were killed all the same." He put the book back and crossed his arms over his chest and leaned against the edge of the bookcase.

"If you do not mean sin, then what do you mean?" Amara carried her dustpan to the garbage bin, pretending to ignore his remark about her fellow sisters from centuries ago who'd been condemned to die. No doubt he wanted to hurt her, but she refused to let him see her pain.

The devil watched her, his dark eyes hot and dangerous.

"A soul can be pure when a mortal loves another more than his or her own life. Diana is the only soul to ever make a deal with me to save someone else."

That surprised Amara. "Surely there have been others."

"I'm sure that people exist who would die for the ones they love, but giving oneself to me? No one has ever done that before. I find her...interesting." He paused at the counter and looked at the glass display cases. "The little present you gave her was charming. Ineffective, but charming."

Amara's face heated. "It won't work?"

"No, not on me. Lower demons, of course, but fallen angels? Never. We Fallen may be barred from heaven, but part of our grace is still there—not the part that allows us back through the pearly gates, but enough to fool little party tricks like the kind with blessed talismans. When I lost my wings, I thought it was all gone, but it turns out that there's a tiny bit still inside me, alive and kicking." He held up his thumb and index finger as he spoke, pinching a tiny portion of the air together.

Grace. Amara couldn't believe it. The devil still had some small bit of the grace of God inside him?

"I will let you keep your life, Amara. I find you delightful. You're terrified of me, but you haven't shown it once. Humans like you are good to have around. It's no fun to play chess with heaven when the other team has only pitiful pawns."

Amara kept her mouth shut. She would not thank the devil for sparing her life.

"If Diana does visit you again, you may ease her concerns. I don't tend to break my favorite toys." He removed a beautiful crucifix from the glass case and examined it in the gold lights of the chandelier hanging above her counter. Amara held her breath.

"As long as she does not rescind the contract, nor does she resist my demands, she will be released from our deal in three months' time. Of course, when she dies, her soul is mine. Forever. But we mustn't let her worry about that, not when she's got about seventy or so years to enjoy life."

"But she will be changed, won't she? When you're done with her?"

The devil smiled, his eyes now cold and black as obsidian. "Oh yes, most certainly. She'll be corrupted, a soul destined straight for hell when the time is right. But you may pick up the pieces of whatever is left if you feel particularly noble."

"I will," she promised.

With another smirk, he walked toward the door and left.

A sigh of relief escaped Amara. "Oh, Lord." She muttered a soft prayer. If the devil planned to visit her more often, she'd have to think about relocating. She paused as she replayed the conversation in her head. Two things about their encounter felt off. The devil had seemed concerned about Amara, a mere mortal, interfering with a contract. He'd also agreed to let Diana go after three months, at least until it was her time to die. That was...*merciful.*

The last time she checked, the devil was not supposed to be merciful.

"YOU DIDN'T KILL HER?" ANDRAS ASKED AS LUCIEN WALKED into the shadows by the closed shop and left.

"No," Lucien said. "She is more useful alive."

"How so?" Andras kept pace with him as they walked toward the parking lot. Lucien felt like moving at the moment, not flitting about with a flick of his thoughts.

"I want Diana to come to me willingly. I do not want her becoming frightened and revoking the contract. Having the pure soul we need is too important. The more she wants me and the darkness, the quicker I can claim her for the gates. If she feels she can run to Amara and find some comfort, then she will be ready to face my desires rather than run from them. So Amara is not to be touched. I want you to ensure her protection."

Andras let out a sigh. "If word gets out we're protecting a white witch..."

"All hell would break loose?" Lucien joked.

"Possibly." Andras frowned.

Lucien slapped him on the back. "Lighten up, old friend. After millennia, I have finally found something that interests me again. This is a cause for celebration. Meet me at the club in half an hour. We will find some succulent humans to slake our lust."

At this, Andras smiled. "It has been too long since either of us indulged."

"Indeed." Lucien could spend days in bed with women,

taking them over and over, never tiring of it. Every position, every toy, every fantasy—he'd done it all.

Andras vanished.

Lucien slid his hands into his pockets and walked along the darkened streets. Night was a time of beauty, a time when shadows ruled and the chill of the breeze rustled the limbs of trees in a way that made one's hair stand on end. Midnight was his favorite time, even though it was a few hours away. When clocks chimed away the twelfth hour, the battle between night and day was completely equal, giving the world a sense of balance, a sense of beauty, a sense of peace.

It had been so long since he had felt peace.

After the fall, he'd mistakenly thought that he would find it, but he had not. His shoulder blades itched, the knotted scars the only imperfect part of him. They always ached when he thought too long about the wings that had once been there.

You can never taste heaven again, not fully. He knew that, yet as he sealed the bargain with Diana he had tasted heaven. *Her* heaven. And he wanted more, was desperate to feel that peace, that bliss her lips had given him. If kissing her, merely kissing her, had been that strong, bedding her would be explosive. There was an irony to it all—the more he would take her to see heaven again, the more he would be condemning her to hell. But that was the bargain, and she had agreed.

He knew Andras would be waiting for him, but he didn't return to the club right away. First he closed his eyes and honed his focus on Diana. He could see inside her apartment, her...cat? The white-and-orange creature stared at him, his ears flattened. People assumed cats were evil, familiars of the devil, but it wasn't true. Cats were a bane to a demon's existence, and they often didn't like fallen angels. They could see and sense the unnatural presence of creatures like him.

"Seth, what's the matter?" Diana came out of her bedroom dressed in boxers and a loose T-shirt.

The cat ignored her, his feline glare still on Lucien. Lucien flipped his middle finger at the cat, and it hissed and sprinted into the bedroom. Diana shook her head and sighed before she went to the kitchen. Lucien followed her, an invisible undetectable presence.

Diana put a kettle on her stove and prepared a tea bag in a mug. As she waited for the water to boil, there was a stark loneliness to her face that puzzled him. He honestly didn't spend much time around mortals, not like this. He was either torturing them, making deals, or banging them in his bed.

She is to be my toy. I am allowed to watch her, to see what she's up to when I'm not around to pull her strings and make her dance like a marionette.

The kettle whistled, and Diana turned off the stove and poured a cup of tea, and then she took the cup to the couch and settled in with a blanket and a book. He eased down onto the edge of the couch arm and leaned over to study the book she opened. He frowned. A vampire romance.

Ugh. There was nothing romantic about those bloodsucking, brooding immortals. Fallen angels were far more interesting. When they bit a lover in bed, it was for fun and not for sustenance.

"Don't worry, Diana. I'll show you how much fun we can have in bed," he whispered. She shivered and pulled the blanket up tighter. She had heard him, the barest hint of his sensual promise.

"Sleep well," he added with a low laugh and left her to dream about him.

༄

HE WAS THERE, IN HER ROOM. A DARK SHADOW IN THE

corner with glowing red eyes. Diana tried to open her mouth to scream, but nothing came out. The shadow moved closer, manifesting itself into him, Lucien Star, in his black suit with a blood-red tie. He stared down at her on the bed, and then very slowly he reached for the covers, drawing them back to expose her. She was naked, her pajamas gone, and he was looking over her body with a satisfied smirk.

It was a dream, she knew it was, had to be...yet it felt all too real as his hand gripped her throat tightly enough to send new shivers of dread through her.

"Such a pretty little thing, and all mine." Still grasping her throat, he leaned down and brushed his lips over hers. Heat exploded from that kiss, burning her up with an inner fire. Wetness pooled between her thighs.

"How will you resist me? When I fuck you into oblivion, little mortal? Will you shriek my name as I thrust my cock deep into you? Will you moan when I take your ass? I have a thousand ways I want to take you. And you will enjoy every second of it, won't you?" He sank his teeth into her bottom lip hard enough that she tasted blood. He tugged on it while he continued to squeeze her throat just enough that she feared she wouldn't be able to breathe.

"No!" she screamed and jolted up in bed. The covers fell down around her, and she reached to cover her naked body... but she wasn't naked any longer. She was clothed again, and the shadow Lucien was gone.

I was dreaming. It was all a dream. She winced as she licked her lip and tasted blood.

❧ 4 ❧

Wednesday came without much fanfare until it was time to take her father home from the hospital. The dreams of Lucien came every night, but that was all they were. Dreams. So she focused on her parents. Diana still couldn't believe it—her father was really going home. He'd been given doctor's orders that he rest, and now he was looking better than he had in years.

Diana spent the day with him and her mother, helping her father settle into his old routines. It was still instinctive for her to try to help her father climb the stairs to his bedroom, but he didn't need her help at all. The ragged edge to her emotions from two years of worry was softening. Had he really been this healthy once? With a flush of color in his cheeks and a twinkle in his eyes? She'd forgotten the man he'd once been. It was hard to remember after so many nights in the hospital, so many tubes, tests, and machines all trying to keep him alive.

Diana waited outside his room for him to change out of his hospital sweatpants into jeans and a polo shirt. Then he returned with her to the kitchen, where her mother was checking on a pot roast she'd put into the oven that morning. Diana's mouth watered, and she realized she hadn't eaten pot roast in ages. It had been her dad's favorite food because the smells would fill the house for hours while it cooked, and neither she nor her mother could stand the smell without him there to enjoy it.

"Everything okay?" Janet asked as they entered the kitchen.

Hal winked at her. "Everything's great, hon. Smells fantastic. You know it's so funny, after all that chemo, nothing smelled or tasted good, but damn if I don't smell that roast now and it's making me hungry." Hal joined his wife by the kitchen counter and leaned in to hug her from behind, giving her a kiss on the cheek. Janet blushed and Diana turned away, smiling, but feeling a little shy at witnessing something so private between her parents. They'd been suffering together for two years, and now...now things were good again. She was terrified to believe it was all true, that her dad was healthy again, because if he wasn't, she and her mother couldn't go through that again.

"We have a contract, Diana. He's safe as long as you abide by the terms." Lucien's voice stirred inside her mind, and she shuddered.

"Leave me alone," she hissed under her breath.

"You're mine, remember? Or do I need to show up in person and remind you just what is at stake if you break the contract."

"Diana, let's go for walk," her father said. His hopeful expression was too much to ignore. Getting outside would do her some good. Get her mind off deals with the devil.

"Sure, sounds fun. Mom?" Diana reached for her light jacket.

Her mother smiled and nodded at the door to her . "You

guys go on. I have some catching up to do. The laundry won't fold itself, and I've got a million emails from the office to answer."

Diana knew her mother had taken a lot of time off work recently when it became clear that her father wasn't going to get better.

Her father put on his coat, and Diana followed him outside.

"Can you believe this? Wonderful sunshine, light breeze, fresh air." Hal's joy was infectious, and Diana couldn't resist basking in the glow of his happy mood. He looked like he was two seconds away from skipping down the sidewalk like a little kid, and she couldn't help but grin. Was this really happening? She and Hal walked to the park, just like they used to do on the weekends before he'd fallen ill. Yet part of her feared this was all an illusion. She'd heard that some people with cancer suddenly got better before relapsing and dying shortly after. Maybe the treatments the doctors had been trying worked and...

She shook the thought off. She knew the truth deep down. But it didn't mean she had to face it—or the devil— today. Today was about her father coming home.

Thinking about her bargain with Lucien was something she could put off for another day. Yet she found her thoughts straying back to him—and the increasingly erotic dreams she had—over and over. In her dreams, he would do things to her, dirty things that made her cry out with pleasure, and she'd wake up trembling, her panties soaked with her arousal. She was going to have to meet him, *sleep* with him in just two days. She was so not ready for that. No one could be ready to have sex with the devil, right?

"You seem preoccupied," her dad said when they reached the end of the street.

Diana glanced at the cute row of houses, some with the proverbial white picket fences, others with gardens and big trees. She'd always loved his neighborhood. It was the place she'd grown up, the place she called home and felt safe.

"I guess I am a little." She wished she could talk to him about everything on in her mind, but she couldn't. You didn't ever tell your father that you'd sold yourself to the devil to save him.

"I know you and your mother are worried about this cure being temporary, but even the doctor said he couldn't find any evidence of the tumors."

"I know," she admitted. She never really kept secrets from her parents, not big ones, but a bargain with the devil was as big as it could get, and she couldn't tell her father about her deal. Guilt ate away at her, but this was one thing she had to keep a secret, even if it hurt her to lie.

"Talk to me, Di." Her father's gentle but focused gaze dug the knife deeper in her heart. "You never were afraid to talk to me before."

They crossed the street and headed to the small park. A few children ran about the sand pit and climbed on brightly colored equipment. She and her father stopped at the edge of the sand pit and watched the kids play for a minute.

"Dad, have you ever agreed to do something you didn't want to in order to make sure something else, something good happened?"

"Hmm...that depends. Is what you're doing going to hurt someone else?"

"No! No, of course not...except maybe me."

Hal sat down on the park bench, and she joined him. He looked away, a frown curving his lips down.

"What kind of hurt are you talking about? Because few things in life are worth getting hurt over."

"Maybe *hurt* isn't the right word." A little girl climbed up

the ladder and then went down the slide, giggling. The innocence of the child and her joy soothed Diana. "I think it's
more that what I do might be wrong."

"Unethical? Illegal or immoral?"

"Maybe immoral," she said. "But it only affects me. No
one else." Her father's face morphed before her eyes, the
curiosity ebbing away as his eyes narrowed and his lips turned
down at the corners. Guilt gnawed at her insides for worrying
him, and she nearly took her question back, but then he
spoke in his thoughtful way.

"I guess you have to ask yourself if the price of betraying
yourself is worth whatever good comes out of it." He put a
hand on her shoulder, squeezing gently. "I know you think
you have to protect yourself and keep secrets sometimes, but
let me help. I can offer sage advice—that's the benefit of
being a parent." He winked at her, and she smiled.

"I know. I know how supportive you and Mom are." They
were the kind of parents most kids would die to have. But the
bargain she'd made wasn't something they would ever understand. *This is something I must do alone.* "But I promise everything is fine, okay? If I had a real problem, I promise I'd come
to you for help."

Hal sighed and closed his eyes, tilted his head back, and
breathed deeply. The lines of worry were gone, and he looked
years younger. It was strange to see him looking so good and
healthy again after everything. The grief that had weighed her
down was fading the more she looked at him.

"You're really feeling better?" she asked.

He nodded. "It's like I had a black cloud all over me,
choking me, pressing me down. Every bone hurt, every
muscle was so inflamed that I could barely think past the
pain. But now? It's like I'm twenty years old again. I feel
strong, I feel..." He fisted his hands. "I feel like me again."

If it really was because of the bargain she had made,

Diana would pay any price for this, to see her father happy and healed. Even if that meant facing the reality of what her dark and frightening erotic dreams with Lucien promised.

They remained on the park bench for another half an hour before they decided to walk home. Her mother was waiting and had the pot roast ready. Diana felt like she was a teenager again, being home with her parents and just sharing dinner, but when her mother offered her old room upstairs for the night, she waved a hand.

"I think I ought to head home. Seth has been acting weird lately, and I don't want to leave him alone for too long."

"Weird?" Her mother paused in the act of putting some of the dishes from the sink into the dishwasher.

"Yeah." Diana leaned against the kitchen counter. "He's been hissing at the air and running away from nothing. It's just weird." She was pretty sure she knew what was upsetting her cat, but she wasn't about to tell her parents that the devil was visiting her in dreams at night and fucking her into oblivion.

"Huh?" Her mother shrugged. "Cats," she said, as if that one word was enough.

"You leaving, honey?" Her father came into the kitchen and joined her mom by the sink.

"Yeah. I'm heading out. I'll see you guys in a few days, okay?" Diana hugged them before she left the house and got into her car. She was so lost in her thoughts that she didn't remember driving the entire way back to her apartment.

This time when she pulled into the driveway of her apartment complex, she knew immediately that something was *off*. Like that weird sense she was being watched. She climbed the stairs to her apartment, wanting to escape the strange feeling, but as she turned into the hallway toward her door, she froze. There, on her welcome mat, was a black velvet box tied with a crimson ribbon.

"What the"

She picked up the box, studying it. It had a solid weight, and she gave it a cautious shake. She heard some indistinct rustling. Diana took the package and tucked it under her arm before she unlocked the door and slipped inside. Seth rushed up to meet her, but she removed the box from under her arm, and he hissed and flattened his ears.

"Oh!" In a flash, a thought struck her. The cat had reacted to the letter from Lucien's attorney and now this box. Was he reacting to...the devil? If that was the case, had he been here last night when she was reading?

"Oh God..." What else had he seen? *Holy crap, can he see me naked?*

A metallic taste filled her mouth, and she panicked.

Calm down. This might be a good thing. Seth could be my canary in a coal mine. If he's freaking out at nothing, it might mean I have an invisible visitor. That would be good to know...I think.

Diana set the box on her kitchen table and slowly pulled at the red satin ribbon. Lifting the lid on the box, she gasped. A red-and-cream lace dress was delicately folded in the charcoal-gray tissue paper. There was also a pair of black heels, incredibly sexy ones, with a black leather strap that went around her ankles and a strap across her toes.

A velvet pouch resting on the dress contained diamond earrings in the shape of teardrops and a diamond choker. By the clarity of the stones and the weight of it in her palms, it felt way too real to be costume jewelry.

"Holy shit." Diana dropped the jewelry back into the pouch and picked up the note card that was tucked between the shoes.

Diana,

You will wear this outfit on Friday night. Do not disobey. Remember, pleasing me means your father remains alive.

Sincerely,

Lucien Star

Seth crawled out from under the couch and stared at the bag with an all too feline look of contempt. Diana put everything in the box and put the lid back on it. Then she carried it over to her coat closet, set it on the top shelf, and closed the door. She hoped, perhaps foolishly, that if it was out of sight, she could somehow forget it until Friday.

For the next few hours, Diana busied herself with her summer classes on macroeconomics. But her gaze kept drifting back to the closet and the box.

Do not look at it. No doubt that's what he wants. Have you all upset over it and lose focus on what matters. And right now, homework matters.

Another half hour passed, and with a frustrated little growl she retrieved the box and stepped into her bedroom. Seth followed, his glowing amber eyes disapproving as he leapt on the bed and sat like a sphinx.

"I'm just going to try it on. There's no way he could know my size, and it will be fun to send this back telling him that."

She stripped out of her jeans and sweater before she pulled on the red-and-cream lacy dress. It fit snugly, but it wasn't tight. The fabric seemed to move with her body. The sleeves were cold-shoulder in design, which was nice. She put on the heels and the jewelry next, just to get the full effect, and then she walked over to the full-length mirror and gazed at herself in awe. The dress hugged her body like a second skin except for the skirt, which flared in a movie star sort of way. A dress like this made a girl feel gorgeous and sexy.

Diana fingered the diamond choker against her throat, feeling for a moment like a collared dog, a pet that belonged to the king of hell. Most of her cringed in revulsion at the thought, but there was a tiny, soft voice in the back of her mind whispering thoughts she always did her best to ignore.

What will he be like in bed? What pleasures will he show you?

She didn't want to know, at least that's what she told herself. She stared at her reflection in the mirror for a long while, doubts assailing her. Friday night was only two days away.

Just two days before she spent time with the devil.

WHAT HATH NIGHT TO DO WITH SLEEP? —
JOHN MILTON, PARADISE LOST

T *he first midnight*

IT WAS TIME.

Diana fastened the diamond earrings on her earlobes with trembling fingers, betraying her nerves. All day long she'd counted the minutes. Seconds had crawled by, and yet time ran forward in an instant and she faced the myth-turned-reality of her bargain. The lace dress slid seductively against her skin. It brought back vivid memories of her dreams about Lucien touching her. Her body flushed with treacherous heat, and she hated herself for reacting to him and the dreams. But damn...he made her so hot, so hungry with his hands, his mouth. His entire body seemed designed to tempt a woman to leave all rationality behind.

And tonight she was going to be with him for real. Dread and fascination warred within her, and she drew in a shaky breath.

It's going to be okay. It has to be.

Headlights flooded the driveway below her second-story window, and she knew, without even looking, that the car had arrived. Precisely on time. *The devil's in the details...*

Grabbing an overnight bag, she hesitated at the threshold of her apartment. The note hadn't said *not* to bring anything, but if he expected her to stay a whole night, she damn well wouldn't be dropped off in the morning wearing this dress, which was nothing more than an exquisite glorified negligée.

Stiffening her spine and her resolve, she gave Seth one last scratch behind the ears and shut the apartment door behind her, head high as she made her way down the stairs and out the front door to the waiting car.

She hesitated a moment, knowing that once she got into the car, she couldn't go back. Finally she gripped the handle, opened the door, and tossed her bag in. The driver made no chivalrous move to open her door or help her with her bag. But that made sense. The devil probably didn't employ nice guys.

She buckled herself in and peered at the driver through the space between the two front seats, her heart pounding as she knew she was one step closer to meeting Lucien again.

"Welcome, Ms. Kingston."

The driver seemed so normal—medium build, gray eyes, not unattractive. He caught her eyes in the rearview mirror and smiled slightly. Was he a demon? Or a human like her?

Now that she was thinking about it, what did demons look like? Could they appear normal? It would seem they could. After all, they were supposed to deceive humans, right? For a few minutes she was able to distract herself from the idea of sleeping with Lucien by focusing on even scarier ideas like demons existing in the world.

The driver didn't interrupt her thoughts as he drove through the bustling city of Chicago. Suburbia turned to urban warehouses and buildings, and the sky kept darkening from purple to endless black outside of the glow of streetlights.

And then suddenly, the boom of music brought her out of her musings, and the car stopped in front of a club. Hellfire Rising. Of course, the name of the devil's home.

The driver broke the silence while he parked the car. "I'll take you inside." He got out of the car, and a flood of loud music, people chatting, and cars honking in traffic filled the interior until he closed the door. Alone and in complete silence, the weight of her decision to go through with her deal pushed down on her shoulders, making her slump. She had one last chance to escape. But then...her father... She didn't dare break her promise to the devil now.

Her door opened, and the cacophony of sound surrounded her again. Diana grabbed her bag, exited quickly, and followed the driver inside the club only to discover an empty interior, which made no sense at midnight on a Friday.

Unease prickled down her spine like invisible fingers playing a sinister melody. "Where is everyone?" she asked the driver.

"Mr. Star closed the club tonight because he wishes to have no distractions while you're here." His chuckle was slightly teasing, but there was a look in his eyes that seemed to be...pity?

Diana swallowed hard, her nerves making her edgy, and her knees knocked together.

"This way please. You will use this elevator to reach the penthouse each time you come." The driver took her to a set of gold-and-black elevator doors and pressed the call button. The doors slid open, and the driver came into the elevator with her. He pointed at a flat panel by the door.

"Place your right palm on the scanner, and it will allow you to access his penthouse."

After a moment's hesitation, she reached out and did as he instructed. The panel glowed green beneath her hand, and the elevator doors closed. They rode up ten floors in silence, and she had the sudden urge to laugh. Shouldn't she be going *down* to see the devil?

She wasn't sure what she expected, but the suite of rooms she stepped into was beautiful. The furniture was sleek and dark, the carpets crisp and white. A glass-and-rock fireplace burned in the corner of the main room. It was stunning and seductive. *Did you expect pits of fire and blood everywhere? He may be the devil, but he wants to seduce you, not scare you off.*

"You'll be all right," the driver said behind her, and then he hit the button to take himself back down.

She set her bag down. There was no sign of *him*. She walked into the room and paused when she reached the bookshelves along one wall by a tall, wide window. Several books that appeared more than a hundred years old peeked out from the shelf. Their gold-lettered spines glinted in the firelight. An exquisite grandfather clock in one corner struck midnight as she approached the bookcase.

Dante's *Inferno*. Not a surprise. She read more titles, discovering Edgar Allan Poe, Oscar Wilde's *The Picture of Dorian Gray*, and even a few paperbacks, along with one she'd read, Susan Hills's *The Woman in Black*. The story was poignant, beautiful, and terrifying. She trailed a finger along the spine and then moved farther down the row of mahogany bookshelves.

A glint and a flash of light near the window caught her eye. She found a clear square display case, and the contents left her breathless.

A single white feather hung in the air, floating under the glass. Shimmering particles swirled slowly around the suspended feather like silver dust. Pale creamy moonlight illuminated the snowy feather, mesmerizing her. She gripped the glass and lifted, ready to touch the feather, but a voice from behind her sent her heart racing.

"Rule number one: you must never touch the feather. *Never.*" The bite to his tone made her shiver, not in a good way.

Diana set the glass case down immediately and spun to face the direction she'd heard the voice.

In the shadows of the corner opposite the fireplace, she saw *him* sitting in a black leather armchair. Darkness concealed his face while he calmly trimmed the tip of a cigar with a silver cutter.

"I'm sorry." She glanced back at the feather, and then a wild thought struck her. "Is that yours?" She knew the story from the Bible like anyone else. Lucifer, the brightest morning star, had been an angel before he'd fallen and become the king of hell. This man had once been an *angel.*

"Yes. You must never touch it. It still retains a bit of heaven's powers, and it could be dangerous for a mortal to touch." He closed the cigar cutter and set it aside on a small table by his chair and leaned forward, his face suddenly lit by moonlight and firelight.

He was just as beautiful as she remembered. She still couldn't believe it. Dark hair and dark-brown eyes that seemed to change into obsidian. She couldn't stop looking at his striking, otherworldly features.

"So it's midnight and I'm here." She was proud of how steady her voice sounded, even though her stomach clenched with fear.

"Yes, you are." He rose from his chair and pulled out a lighter from his pocket and lit the cigar.

"You shouldn't smoke. It's bad for your health." The moment she said it, she felt like an idiot. He was a fallen angel, not a human, so most likely he couldn't get lung cancer. But she could.

He drew on the cigar, inhaling slowly, and then he let out a puff of smoke. It danced in the air toward her, and she coughed. A sudden flash of anger at the thought that he wouldn't care about her health made her speak up.

"I guess it doesn't affect you, but I can still get ill from the secondhand smoke." She couldn't believe she was telling him off. It was dangerous.

His sensual lips curved into a smile. He puffed again on the cigar and then set it down into an ashtray on the table beside him, the tip of it still burning red.

"Rule number two. While you are with me between midnight and sunrise, nothing can hurt you, not my cigars, nothing." The arrogance in his tone made her bristle.

"What? But how—"

"Think of it as me pausing your body's clock. Everything will go on as normal, but while you're with me, you're safe from anything that could befall you."

"Anything except...you?" she clarified.

Again that wicked smile that made her insides burn, but it also sent a flash of fear through her that raced like a wildfire. "Yes. Rule number three: while you're with me, you will obey my commands. If I tell you to strip and climb into my bed, you do it."

Oh God...

"Is that what you want me to—"

"No. Not right now. I'll make it clear when I give you an order." He pulled back the sleeve on his left arm and examined his watch.

"I think if we leave now we can make the reservation."

"Reservation?" She stared at him.

"There's a little place on Malibu Beach where I have a cook who prepares quite a meal. He is waiting for us."

"But Malibu is in California, and we're in Illinois."

Lucien walked to a door near the bookshelves and opened

it. Diana's jaw dropped. Beyond the doorway she saw a beach house on a slight hill lit with strings of light.

"But... How...?" She simply pointed at the open doorway. "That's not..."

"Possible?" Lucien held out a hand to her. "Everything is possible. *Everything* so long as you're with me."

Of course it was. He'd healed her father. He had heavenly —or maybe hellish—powers. A quick trip to Malibu was just par for the course, right? She swallowed down a hysterical laugh.

Diana stared at the invitation of his waiting hand, knowing she couldn't walk away. Every doubt and fear was silenced inside her as she remembered her father in the park, the relief, the joy, the pain gone from him. There had been only life and sunlight.

I'll do anything to keep that. She crossed the short distance between her and Lucien and placed her palm in his.

Without another word, he tugged and she followed him to the portal. She stumbled onto the sand and almost tripped. Lucien kept walking, his hand in hers, but she couldn't move because her expensive heels sank into the sand. He sighed and scooped her up in his arms. His sudden possessive hold of her body wasn't frightening, but rather a mixture between thrilling and comforting.

She didn't want to think about why she felt that way, but she shivered and burrowed closer, her heart racing. She wrapped her arms around his neck to stay steady as he walked. The tips of her fingers brushed the silk of his hair at the base of his neck, and she suddenly longed to dig her hands into those dark shiny strands. His body was muscular and warm, with an earthy scent that teased her nose. He was pure temptation and sin, right down to that intoxicating scent.

"I'm sorry I tripped. Heels and sand don't really work."

He didn't say anything for a long while. Then he chuckled, the sound surprisingly pleasant.

"I shall make a note of that for future outings, but I do like the way you look in those heels. They will be even better when I have your legs thrown over my shoulders and those heels are digging into my back."

Diana stiffened.

"Whatever you're thinking, I assure you that sharing my bed will be one of the best experiences of your life."

I doubt that. She had a bucket list of a hundred things she wanted to do, and sex with the devil was not on that list. Hell, sex in general was not on the list. The few boys she'd dated in high school and college had been nice, but she felt like she'd missed that spark that everyone talked about. Maybe it wouldn't be terrible to be with him. She could survive three months of mediocre sex.

Lucien carried her up a stone stairway that had been carved into the rocks. They headed toward the house which sat on the rocky hill. He set her down at the base of the stairs and brushed the sand off her feet before they climbed up to the house. It was illuminated with twinkling lights, and the ocean below crashed into the shore in a peaceful rhythm. Diana had always loved the ocean and the salty sea breeze. Something about the briny smell calmed her like nothing else.

The house Lucien led her to was a stone-and-glass structure that was modern and beautiful. It would probably be stunning in the daytime. They walked around the side of the house until they reached the front. Lucien opened the door, and she came in after him while he held it for her.

"Henry?" Lucien called as they walked straight into a kitchen that would've inspired any cook's fantasies. There were stainless-steel countertops and open shelves painted blue and white with a coastal seashore charm. There was a massive island in the middle with a blue spun glass fruit bowl filled with gleaming red apples. She glanced toward Lucien for a moment, wondering if the red apples were there to make a point. But he wasn't looking at her; he was focused on the chef, who was hard at work.

Henry was a middle-aged man, and he was standing in front of the main counter, drizzling a sauce over some sautéed vegetables. He smiled when he saw them.

"Mr. Star, the first course is ready. You arrived at just the right time."

"Excellent. Henry, this is Ms. Kingston, my guest for the evening."

"Hi." Diana waved at the cook, trying to act normal. It was just dinner. Dinner with the devil, who'd carried her across a Malibu beach and promised to fuck her senseless after dinner. Yeah, no reason at all to be nervous.

"It's a pleasure to meet you." His warmth was obvious and genuine. Diana couldn't help but wonder how Henry had met the devil. Did he have a bargain too? If she had a chance to ask him, she would.

"Why don't you both have a seat, and I'll bring in the first course," Henry suggested as he picked up a wooden pepper grinder and lightly dusted the two dishes.

"You heard him." Lucien held out his arm to Diana, and the courtly gesture surprised her. They passed through the kitchen into a lovely dining room. Tall-backed black leather chairs and a rustic dark wooden table set for two. Lucien pulled her chair out for her, and after she sat, he pushed her in. Then he took a seat next to her.

Henry served the first course, an Asian blend of sautéed vegetables. Then he poured two glasses of what he called a full-bodied red and presented it to them before returning to the kitchen.

Diana lifted her glass and was about to drink when she

saw Lucien swirl his glass and inhale slowly, all the while watching her. Then he took a drink.

"It's not poisoned." He chuckled when she still hesitated.

"It's not poison I'm worried about," she said as she realized he could put all sorts of drugs into her drink. The man could become invisible, for goodness' sake.

Lucien let out a deep laugh. "Oh, my dear Ms. Kingston, I'm the devil—I don't need to drug anyone. It's rather like cheating. I chose you because of the challenge you present. To seduce a pure soul to the dark side? What a delicious temptation."

"So you're not going to..." She choked down the word that had been lurking in the back of her mind.

"Force you?" He seemed genuinely displeased at her assumption. "No. There's no fun in that. But you will surrender to me, and the power you will give up to me will be my best victory yet." His displeasure turned to confidence, but she knew she wouldn't just surrender.

She relaxed a little and finally allowed herself to taste the wine. It was a rich cabernet. "Do you mind if I ask you something?" She picked up her fork and tried a bit of her appetizer. Spices exploded on her tongue. *God, Henry knows how to cook.*

"Ask away. I'm willing to lay bare for you." Lucien's innuendo wasn't lost on her. He took a few bites as well and made a soft, contented sound that sent shivers through her. He made it sound...*sexual*.

"So the paperwork from your attorney said you go by Lucien Star. But you're Lucifer, right?"

Lucien stroked the stem of his wine glass as he contemplated his answer. "I've been the king of hell for a very long time. It can be a dull, repetitive existence. I wanted to have a life outside the business."

A life outside hell? She couldn't imagine the devil wanting

anything to do with anything other than hell. But she was wrong. She couldn't resist her increasing curiosity.

"So Lucien Star, like the Morning Star?" Diana finished off the rest of her food and waited to hear the devil explain himself.

"I've always loved and hated that name." His voice softened, and his gaze drifted away from her.

"Why do you hate it?"

"To be called your father's brightest star and then be cast into the darkness where nothing can shine?" He gripped the wine glass so hard the glass shattered. Diana flinched and rushed to wipe up the mess.

"Leave it," he barked and snapped his fingers. The shattered glass vanished, and a new one appeared in its place.

Diana dropped her wine-soaked napkin onto the table, frowning. She'd never really had anyone yell at her before, and she'd only been trying to help. He may be Lucifer, but he wasn't going to treat her like that.

"You shouldn't yell at me. I was only trying to help."

She met his glare bravely, and he sighed. "My apologies, Ms. Kingston. I'm afraid discussing anything that relates to my *fall* makes me disagreeable."

He sounded so formal, even more so than usual. She didn't know him at all. Could one know the devil? At least she was learning something. *Never mention the fall.*

"I'm not interested in discussing myself. I'd much rather learn about you."

"Really?" She couldn't believe that. He only wanted to corrupt and seduce her.

"That surprises you?" He leaned forward, his eyes holding her to the spot. "Why wouldn't I be interested in getting to know you, a pure soul and a ripe peach ready for plucking?"

Diana sucked in a breath. She would have been furious seconds before, but the way he spoke, it wasn't an insult, it was a desire. The inferno in his gaze reminded her all too clearly of those hot nights in her dreams where he'd acted like the seductive villain she'd expected him to be tonight. Yet he was being far too gentlemanly tonight. What was his plan? What was the devil up to? It was obvious he was hungry for her, and she, as much as she wished to deny it, was hungry too.

Henry entered the room with two new plates and set them down in front of Lucien and Diana before he removed the empty appetizer plates.

"Mustard chicken, lemon pasta, and a lemon vinaigrette sauce with dill," he announced.

"It looks amazing, Henry. Thank you," Diana said.

Once the cook returned to his kitchen, Diana tasted the entrée, and this time she moaned.

"See? You were judging me earlier—I saw that look you gave me—but some food is good enough that it makes you moan. Some food comes close to being better than sex."

"Close?" she asked.

He grinned wickedly. "Nothing is better than sex, at least when it's done well." The way he said this made her feel like he was taunting her.

"Hmm," she murmured, not agreeing. Sex had always been pleasant before, but she couldn't imagine sex with him would be good, because he was the devil. Yet the way he was looking at her, with that sexy, smoldering gaze that warned her he knew just what she was thinking and couldn't wait to prove her wrong...

That was terrifying.

"You didn't think those dreams you had were just your imagination, did you?" he asked.

She stopped breathing. The dreams. She wanted to forget and yet relive those dark, forbidden fantasies over and over. They had made sex feel overpowering, all-consuming.

"Well?" he demanded, his tone a little darker.

"I...guess I hoped they were."

Lucien put a hand on her leg under the table, his warm palm sliding slowly up her thigh, pushing her dress out of the way until he reached her mound. She tried to scoot her chair back, but he reached up and gripped the back of it, stopping her from retreating.

"Everything I did to you, everything you *begged* me to do, that was only the beginning." His fingertips brushed the seam of her panties, caressing her clit, and she clenched her thighs together automatically, unable to stop reacting to his touch and the memories...or the dreams of how it felt when his body was between her thighs, his weight pressing down on her. He'd controlled her in the dreams, dominated every part of her until she couldn't remember who she was. All she could think about was him and the exquisite pleasure he gave her.

Her body burned like a fire in winter. She wanted to view him coldly, dispassionately, but she couldn't. She kept trying to figure out what made him tick, what he was thinking, and what that look in his eyes meant. Diana would promise far more than was wise if he would let her glimpse who he really was.

He slowly removed his hand from between her legs, making it clear that he was in control, that her body was his to touch as he pleased. The thought turned her on and terrified her at the same time.

"Finish your dinner. We want to get to dessert. That's always the best part."

She ate her entrée in silence, enjoying every bite despite feeling the weight of his gaze. But by the time Henry brought out some type of marbled cheesecake, she had to agree with Lucien. Dessert was the best part. She glanced up at him, unable to ignore his intense focus any longer.

"Diana, I want you to tell me one thing about you that no

one knows," Lucien said just as she finished her dessert. She set her fork down and swallowed.

"I...don't know." She couldn't think of anything.

Lucien leaned over and cupped her chin, their gazes locked, and he repeated his question, his sinful voice seeming to put her in a trance. A funny feeling, like being weightless, took over, and she couldn't seem to stop from speaking.

"I...like to read romance novels. My mom thinks that they're silly, but I love them." It wasn't just the steamy sex scenes that had fascinated her, but the deep, emotional connection the hero and heroine formed by the end of the book. She'd longed for that all her life.

Lucien's finger slowly dropped from her chin, and he rested his head in his hand, studying her thoughtfully.

"Most people..." He paused, his dark eyes slowly starting to glow red. "Most people tell me something dark, something forbidden. But not you."

Diana's heart pounded. She had forbidden desires just like everyone, but she didn't linger on them. Suddenly she could feel something inside her head, an odd sifting, as though she couldn't control her thoughts, and the memories that she kept on the surface were shoved away as the walls around her darkest fantasies were attacked. *He* was inside her head. Digging. Diana slammed her walls up even higher, struggling to grasp memories of happy times and throw them at the presence in her head, and the sifting feeling slowed...then stopped.

"You're going to be a most interesting toy."

"I'm *not* a toy." Diana threw her napkin onto the table and got up. She didn't care if he wanted her to stay seated. She needed fresh air. Rushing outside to the patio doors behind her, she stopped when she reached the railing on the deck and faced the sea. Breathing in the scent, she was calmed at once and barely flinched when Lucien came up behind her.

He placed one hand on her left hip and leaned in to whisper in her ear.

"You *are* a toy, Diana. *My* toy." His tongue flicked against her earlobe, and a shiver rolled through her.

"Remember, my sweet, that is the bargain you made." His hand pressed into her hip, the touch anchoring her down into a pit of darkness where a wildness dwelt. "Give in, Diana." His voice was like honey, slow and sweet, sliding over her and blocking out the sound of the surf. "Don't fight the way you feel. I know you find me attractive, that I arouse you. I see it in your eyes, the way they shimmer with heat."

She opened her eyes, leaned back, and was caught in his gaze.

"You want to know what it would be like to be with me? Let me show you."

ꙮ 6 ꙮ

I FLED, BUT HE PURSUED—JOHN MILTON,
PARADISE LOST

Diana was falling into darkness, into him. She knew she couldn't resist. She turned around to face him, a tear trailing down her cheek. Diana wasn't scared, she was furious—furious that she wanted him, that she liked the way he talked to her, touched her, made her feel vulnerable. He reached out and wiped it with his thumb and then sucked his thumb into his mouth, moaning softly.

"There is nothing so delicious as a mortal's tears. Shed in love, anger, fear, each one has a different taste. Yours is part anger and part fear." He brushed his thumb over her lips, and she parted them, drawing in a breath, and then he slid his thumb between her lips.

"Suck it," he ordered.

Trembling, she did as he ordered. His other hand slid down her back to cup her bottom, his large palm squeezing her hard. Rather than hurting, his touch felt good, too good. Her channel grew wet, and she clenched her thighs together.

Lucien removed his thumb from her mouth, smiling widely. "What a pretty pet you will be." He took her by the hand before she could speak, and in a blinding flash a portal opened up and they stepped inside. They were back in his apartment above the nightclub in Chicago.

He led her to a room she hadn't seen. A bedroom. She held her breath, her heart racing as she took in the room—the devil's bedchamber. It had a fireplace, several chairs, and a couch, and the bed itself was a California king with gauzy red curtains hanging loosely around the four-poster, more for show than for concealment. It was seductive, alluring...something out of her darkest fantasies, the very ones she'd tried to hide from him.

Lucien leaned back on the edge of his bed and pointed at her.

"Remove your dress."

She reached up to undo the zipper on the side, her hand shaking so hard it took her a few tries. Then she shimmied out of it and slowly let it drop to the floor. She wore a sensible black bra and panties, nothing fancy, and she was glad. She covered her body with her arms until she saw him shake his head. She dropped her arms back down to her sides and looked anywhere but at him.

"Can we just get this over with?" she whispered.

His low chuckle was the opposite of comforting. "My dear, we are just getting started." Lucien removed his coat and draped it over a nearby chair. Then he rolled up the sleeves of his white dress shirt and loosened his red silk tie, sliding it off his neck. She watched in equal parts dread and fascination as he wound the expensive silk around his hands the way a boxer would tape his palms. She held her breath as he tightened the silk and then released it.

"Get on the bed and lie on your back, arms above your head."

Shivering, Diana complied. She walked to the edge of the bed and lowered herself onto the silk sheets and then slid to the center of the bed. He watched her every move. She couldn't stop trembling, and it took every ounce of her self-control not to panic when he captured her wrists and bound them together with his red tie that moments ago had been around his neck. Then he snapped his fingers, and a silver chain materialized in his hand. He looped the chain around the knotted tie and then secured her to the wooden spindles of the headboard.

"You will not move or speak, but you may make any sound you like." He stood beside the bed, and after a moment of staring at her, he eased down onto the bed and leaned over her.

Diana closed her eyes, terrified of whatever he might do. She jerked when his fingertips stroked down her cheek.

"You can't hide from me, Diana. Not even in your own head." His voice was closer, and she could feel his breath as it fell upon her lips. "I can see inside your head while you're here in my world." And then his lips covered hers.

The joining of their mouths was like smoldering heat joining metal. She could not fight that kiss—no hot-blooded woman could. A whimper escaped her when he bit her bottom lip and tugged on it. Flashes of images—wind, clouds, the earth rising up to meet her—made her dizzy and entranced. She was so distracted by his kiss that she didn't immediately realize his hand was sliding up her inner thighs until he gave her left thigh a light smack. The faint sting of pain caused her to jolt, and her eyes opened.

He broke the kiss and stayed where he was, leaning over her. Then he slid his hand up to cup her mound, and he brushed his thumb over her clit through the fabric of her panties. She jolted at the sudden touch and the riotous wave of ecstasy that shot through her. It felt good, so good, and she hated that he was giving her such pleasure.

"You belong to me—never forget that. You exist here

until dawn to serve my pleasures and my needs. Do you understand?"

She nodded, but he frowned. "When you are in my bed, I am your lord and master. Do you understand?"

"Y-yes." The words sent a little electric pulse through her. *Don't let your mind go there.* But it was too late. The dark, secret place in her head was close, too close.

"Very good. Tonight is your first lesson. I will be lenient, just once." He continued to rub circles around her clit with his thumb. "Some nights, I will tease you like this for as long as it amuses me. On other nights, I will take you straight to a flat surface, bend you over, and fuck you until you can't walk. And if you continue to please me, we will explore all those hidden fantasies you think you are hiding from me."

No... He couldn't know about those. They were buried deep in her head, safe even from herself. She hoped.

"You have a strong will, but I can wear you down, weaken your defenses. I have all the time in the world." He moved her panties aside and slipped his index finger into her slick folds, twirling the tip in slow, lazy patterns. She couldn't resist wriggling, and he laughed.

"I told you not to move." He slowly rolled her onto her stomach and tugged her panties down to just below her ass cheeks and spanked her hard three times on each cheek. She'd never been spanked before, and the sudden flush of wet heat filled her with shame. He'd turned her on by striking her, the slight bite of pain too erotic to ignore. Then he pulled her panties back up and rolled her once more onto her back. She winced as her tender bottom touched the bed. He didn't wait long before he was parting her folds again and thrusting his fingers into her. He spoke slowly, watching her face closely as she panted and strained to control her body.

Don't move, can't move. He inserted a second finger into her and licked his lips.

"Damn, you're tight. Like a fucking virgin. It's going to feel so good when I fuck you."

His raw, dirty words made a wild unstoppable heat flood her channel. Her few boyfriends had always been sweet, not dirty, and to her shame she liked the way Lucien was touching her and talking about her, about what he wanted to do to her.

"You like that, don't you?" His murmur of satisfaction caused her to tremble. "You like it rough, but you've never had it like that, have you?" He removed his fingers from her and licked them, grinning the entire time. "Don't worry, I'll make it dark, hard, and dirty for you. You'll never want sweet and slow again."

⚜

LUCIEN WAS BARELY IN CONTROL OF HIMSELF. DIANA proved to be a temptation he couldn't resist. Not that he ever resisted long when it came to getting what he wanted. What was the point? As the king of hell, he could do what he wished, take what he wanted. Denying himself anything was only to prolong the exquisite ecstasy once he had what he wanted. And that was why he decided he would not fuck her, not fully, not tonight. He would torture her, tease her, make her come over and over, but he would not possess her. The fear and anger in her eyes hadn't aroused him. Owning a woman's body and soul when she surrendered them willingly was infinitely more arousing.

He slid off the side of the bed and walked over to the foot. Then he climbed onto the bed, his body moving with the grace of a jaguar as he reached over her, gripping her panties, sliding them slowly down her legs. He dangled the fabric off his finger, letting her see them before he tossed them onto the floor.

"Spread your legs and bend your knees," he commanded.

Diana's eyes closed, and her face darkened with a blush that looked like a glass of merlot. Someday soon she would stop feeling shame about her body and passion. He would coax her into the darkness with him. Lucien knelt between her legs and placed his hands on her inner thighs, holding her open as he gazed down at her exposed sex. She was a pretty pink with a small patch of dark hair. *Natural.* He had been with too many women who changed their bodies to fit the ideal woman of a man's fantasies. Fake tits, Botoxed lips, every bit of hair and fat removed. *Fools, all of them.*

He settled down, crouching now above her belly as he placed soft, heated kisses on her mound. She tensed when he parted her folds farther with exploring fingers. An animal hunger took over as he inhaled her scent, natural, full of need and sex. There was nothing more exquisite than those two scents paired together. Humans could act sophisticated all they liked, but when it came down to it, they were creatures just like any other, driven by needs for safety, sex, and sustenance. Sex was the most powerful.

A delicious shudder ran through her as he bent his head and licked her sensitive folds. The tie bit into the flesh of her wrists as she strained, and he chuckled at the erotic sight of her bound and helpless. She writhed at each lick and intimate touch, spreading her legs for him. He continued to explore her, taste her, his mouth never stopping as he worked on her wet center. A breathy moan escaped Diana, and she threw her head back.

"You're so wet for me, pet. I could lap up your cream for days," he murmured, rubbing his cheek against her inner thigh, knowing the scrape of his beard would rasp against her sensitive skin.

"Please," she whimpered.

"Please what?" he replied before he fastened his lips around the bud of her clit, sucking hard.

The wild, desperate sound she made only fed his hunger. He flicked his tongue against her and then thrust into her over and over, a gentle, tortuously light penetration.

"Please stop," she begged.

"Stop? Does it hurt?" He arched a brow as he glanced up at her face. Her breasts rose and fell with rapid breaths.

"Too...good," she confessed brokenly.

He laughed and bent his head again. He'd always been very good at killing people with pleasure. Not that he would kill Diana, but he would let her get close enough to taste the darkness, taste the end of life as she knew it. That would heighten her orgasm so powerfully that she would melt beneath him.

He shifted so he could play with her while boldly swiping his tongue over her clit. Sliding two fingers into her, he curled them, finding a slightly rough patch on her inner walls deep inside her. The hidden G spot. Her hips bucked, and he pressed down on her stomach, pinning her to the bed. Then he fucked her with his fingers in earnest.

"Take it, baby, take it all and like it," he growled before sucking hard on her clit again.

Her body went taut, and he felt her inner walls clamp down around him as she cried out in shock and pleasure. The fire rolled through her body and into his. He stifled a groan of his own. One of the perks of being an angel, even a fallen one, was feeling the emotions and sensations of humans around them. And right now he could feel every pulse, every throb, and every quiver as she came down from the exquisite high of her climax.

He pulled his fingers free from her, licking them clean before he crawled up her body. He settled his hips between her thighs, uncaring that her wet center rubbed against his trousers. He grasped her wrists with one hand, holding her captive as he pressed her down more deeply into the mattress. Then he brushed the backs of his fingers against her cheek. He looked at her, held her gaze with his, fascinated by the glints of color in her gray eyes. Fear—not of him, but what she'd experienced—shadowed her heavy-lidded, sated gaze.

"You should never fear the pleasure I give you."

She blinked and tried to turn her face away, but he didn't let her.

"Don't fight me, *embrace* me." *Embrace the darkness.* He lowered his head to hers. He kissed her slowly at first, teasing her mouth before he let go of his control. He devoured her will to resist, consuming her with his violent need to dominate. Her body writhed beneath his as he rocked his hips, rubbing his pelvis against hers over and over. The need to fuck her almost overpowered him, but he clung to his sanity...barely.

His lips moved savagely over hers. The more he demanded, the more she gave, and then his mind filled with bright piercing light like a shaft of sunlight breaking into the darkness of a cave. Diana's mind flooded with images, with memories, and he was helpless to stop it.

Cool water danced up to her toes, and she squealed in delight, running through the wet sand as waves rolled in.

He couldn't stop it as the images changed again. *Flames on a set of five candles flickered, and wax dripped down the colorful sides as voices sang "Happy Birthday" all around her. She dipped her tiny little finger into the icing nearest her, giggling.*

He could taste her, taste the cake, feel the sea, and he shivered, trying to pull free, but she wrapped her legs around his waist, holding his body down on top of hers.

Her kisses were dangerous. There was too much joy, too much happiness. It reminded him of his grace and heaven. He wasn't supposed to feel this. Pleasure and pain, yes. But not everything in between. Lucien tore his mouth from hers, gasping. She relaxed beneath him, her lashes fanning over her cheeks as she closed her eyes.

"Diana?" he murmured.

"Hmm?" She sounded drowsy, and he had no desire to wake her. He slid off her body and walked to the bathroom, wetting a towel in the sink. Then he returned to his bed and opened her legs, cleaning her between her thighs. Then he freed her wrists from the chain and the tie, tossing them to the floor. Diana moved, rolled onto her side, burying her face into the pillow. A soft sigh escaped her, and in moments she was asleep.

Lucien stared at her, stunned. No woman had ever fallen asleep on him. *Ever*. He wasn't quite sure what to do. After a long moment, he retrieved a red velvet throw and covered her with it, tucking it up to her chin. Then he walked to his liquor cabinet and poured a glass of Speyside scotch. He downed the glass and refilled it before he returned to his bed and leaned against one of the posts at the foot, nursing his drink while studying Diana as she slept. His new pet had surprised him in more ways than he expected. He scrubbed a hand over his jaw, still able to taste the blue icing on the cake from her memories. As an angel, he had a limited set of senses. He could taste, smell, feel everything a human could, but it was rather faded, like an old photograph left too long in the sun. When he kissed Diana, the tastes, smells, and sensations had exploded through him with brilliant clarity.

It frightened him—because it shouldn't be possible.

"What did you do to me?" he asked, but the little mortal didn't answer. She slept so deeply, not even the devil could claim her thoughts.

He would let her sleep until dawn. Next time she wouldn't have it so easy. One orgasm was not enough, not enough for *him*.

Next time, I will take what I want.

☙❧

Sunlight colored the backs of Diana's eyelids with gold. She stirred, blinking slowly as the world around her came into focus. She lay in a massive king-size bed, and red gauzy drapes shimmered in the light coming in from the window. She rolled onto her back and winced as pain twinged her wrists. She lifted one arm up and grimaced at the sight of the slight purple bruising around them. As she moved her legs, she felt velvet on her bare skin.

"What the..." She lifted the blanket and blinked in shock as she saw she wore only a bra and nothing else.

Last night flooded back to her, and she jerked the blanket up to her chin, expecting Lucien to jump out at her from the shadows. After a moment of fearful glances, she realized she was alone. Diana sat up and peered over the side of the bed. Her dress, shoes, and panties were lying on the floor in a heap. Using the red velvet throw as a toga, she slipped out of bed and retrieved her clothes from her overnight bag by the bed, clutching them to her chest, and then she searched the room until she found the bathroom. She locked herself in while she dressed. Bitter shame weighed her down as she put on her jeans and a shirt. Last night she'd felt sexy and terrified.

Now she felt regret. She'd let the devil touch her, play with her, and then she'd come apart beneath him as he kissed her. And it was only going to get worse. He was going to take her fully next time. She'd tasted the promise of it in his kiss.

Yet despite it all, she'd fallen asleep on him. What had he done while she slept? She had no idea, but he'd covered her with a blanket. That was thoughtful for the devil. Diana stared at her flushed face in the mirror, remembering the feel of him between her thighs, licking, sucking, and then penetrating her with those long, elegant fingers. He'd found some dark hidden spot inside her that sent violent shockwaves of pleasure through her.

And his kiss, those hot, sensual lips on hers... It had been unlike anything she'd ever experienced. When she'd kissed him, she felt like she was falling into darkness, like she couldn't breathe, but she didn't *need* to breathe. Some part of her head screamed that she was dying right there in his arms, but she couldn't have stopped him even if she'd wanted to. She'd been too far gone, swept away to dark horizons by the power of her orgasm and the magnetic pull of his body against hers.

Diana picked up a crystal glass by the sink and filled it with water.

She drank it all, her thirst unquenchable for several seconds. When she set the glass back down, she jumped at the sight of a crisp folded piece of paper. It had not been there a minute ago when she'd picked up the glass. The paper was thick, creamy, and expensive. She opened it up. A message had been scrawled in black ink.

Diana,

Each dawn after I leave you, you are welcome to stay as long as you wish. My driver is downstairs, ready to take you home whenever you like. Until next week, pet, I will taste you on my lips and ache for you. Next time I will not be kind or gentle. I won't stop at using only my fingers and tongue. Be prepared, pet.

Lucien

She shivered with a forbidden pulsing desire. She shouldn't want him, not like that, but her body was quick to betray her. She set the note back down on the bathroom counter and combed her fingers through her hair, trying to tame the wild mess. Then she retrieved her bag from the floor by the bed. She paused for just a moment and glanced back at the single white feather in the square glass case. The morning sunlight made it sparkle enticingly. She couldn't believe it had once belonged to an angel, and not just any angel, but Lucifer himself. Maybe that's what captivated her, the fact that he'd once been one of God's favorite angels. With a slow exhale, she turned back to the elevator.

The elevator door opened, and she pressed the button and rode back down to the ground floor. She met the driver as the doors opened, and he led her out into the empty night-club. She didn't say anything as the driver opened her door for her and she climbed into the black Mercedes. He drove her home and even carried her bag to the door. She smiled at him and thanked him. The man paused, and his solemn face suddenly brightened a little as his lips twitched. Then he left her alone.

She unlocked the door and dropped her bag just inside. Seth trotted out of her room, letting out a trailing meow of greeting. She bent and caught him, cuddling him to her chest and breathing in his scent. He purred and rubbed his furry cheek against hers.

"Oh, Seth..." She was relieved to have something to hold on to, to bury her worries even for just a few seconds.

She put Seth down and headed for the bathroom, strip-ping out of her clothes. She turned on the shower and stepped into the tub and pulled the curtain closed. Hot water burned her skin, and she rubbed every inch of her body, trying to wipe away the feel of him. It was as though he'd imprinted himself on her after what he had done to her. She felt...dirty and *owned* by him. She hated that she liked that feeling even more.

"I need help." She wasn't sure who she spoke to, but she just needed to say it. She eased down in the tub, letting the shower water rain down while she covered her face in her hands. Tears came hard and fast, and she let them. Full-body sobs racked her frame. She felt truly alone.

When her eyes were finally dry and she had no energy left

to cry anymore, she stood and finished washing. Then she dressed and made herself some breakfast. She finally felt calm enough to retrieve her schoolbooks and settled down to work. If there was one thing she could do to get the devil out of her mind it was studying. Seth leapt on the table and kept her company.

Don't think about him. Don't think about what you did with him. Don't...

❧ 7 ❧

YE SHALL BE AS GODS, KNOWING BOTH GOOD
AND EVIL, AS THEY KNOW. - JOHN MILTON,
PARADISE LOST

When Monday morning came, Diana practically bounced in her seat as class started. Professor Belkin, a man in his sixties, had a great sense of humor and made her economics class fun and fascinating. The class was small, only fifteen students, but she liked it that way. She focused on taking summer classes whenever possible so she could finish her degree sooner, and she had access to each teacher on a more intimate level with smaller classes. She smiled as one of her friends, a fellow classmate named Jim, took a seat next to her.

"Today we're going to discuss the principal of trade-offs. In basic language, a trade-off is when you give up one thing in order to get another." Belkin took a dry-erase marker and started writing on the whiteboard behind him. Diana opened a Word document on her laptop and started typing some additional notes. She copied the professor's notes. *Trade-off between efficiency and equity.*

"Definition of *efficiency*." Professor Belkin faced the class and tapped the marker against his chest. "It is the property of society getting the maximum benefits from its scarce resources. The definition of *equity* is the property of distributing economic prosperity fairly among the members of society."

Diana typed the definition while the professor waited, giving the class time to catch up.

"Let's think of some examples. Group yourselves up and discuss." Belkin waved at them.

The classmates she worked with were fun and engaging, and by the end of the exercise she was relaxed and enjoying herself. She almost managed to forget the devil's bargain she'd made...*almost*.

When the class was over, she packed up her bag.

"Hey," someone said, and she glanced up. Jim grinned at her.

"Hi." She couldn't resist smiling back. He was cute in that boy-next-door sort of way, with blond hair and hazel eyes. There was just something sweet about him that made her want to grin.

"I'd love to take you out for coffee and talk about the trade-off chapter homework." His easy smile was so different from Lucien. She felt guilty at the comparison, but it was true.

"Um...okay. Let me finish packing up, and I'll meet you outside."

Jim slung his laptop bag over his shoulder and left the classroom.

"Coffee...with a regular guy." She bit her lip to hide a grin. It sounded *really* nice. Yet she couldn't help but wonder if Lucien might ever be the guy who could do regular coffee. Probably not. For some reason, that left her feeling disappointed. Which she knew was terrible. She should be celebrating her freedom during the week, but it didn't change the fact that she couldn't get the devil out of her mind.

"I THINK YOU HAVE A PROBLEM."

Lucien looked up when Andras walked into his office, interrupting his assessment of the club finances, a task he completed every month though he knew there would not be any monetary worries. He wasn't about to let a bunch of humans stiff him on the cost of doing business.

"What problem?"

"There's an angel sniffing around your woman." Andras took a cigarette lighter out of his pocket and flicked the silver lid open, letting a flame spark to life.

"Diana? She's not my...wait, you said an angel? What angel?" Lucien didn't have women who belonged to him, except where Diana was concerned. She was *his*, and no angel had any right to go and take what was his.

"Where is she?" Lucien demanded.

"Leaving her class. They're grabbing coffee." Andras smirked.

"Coffee?" Lucien growled. "I'll tear his wings off myself."

He closed his eyes, and when he opened them he was standing in the hall outside her classroom at the local university. His skin prickled as he sensed an angel's close proximity.

"Show yourself," he ordered.

Suddenly a young blond-haired man in slacks and a white dress shirt appeared. The shadows of his invisible wings fanned out on the wall behind him.

"Jimiel?" Lucien recognized the angel as one of his brothers from before the fall.

"Lucifer." Jimiel's eyes narrowed, and he tossed his bag to the floor, then assumed a battle stance.

"You're the one sniffing around my woman?" Lucien opened his palms, balls of fire manifesting.

"She's not your woman," Jimiel said, his gaze cool and

aloof. "Diana Kingston is mine. The moment she was born, I was assigned as her earthly guardian."

"Father is up to his old tricks? I thought he gave up the whole 'guardian angel' thing centuries ago." His hands still sparked with flames, and he was hungry to burn the winged idiot to ash. He may have been demoted from angel status, but being elevated to king of hell had some real perks, including smiting angelic assholes like Jimiel.

"For certain mortals, he still assigns angels. Diana is one of those. She is destined to change the world for the better. Her life must be guarded at all times."

Lucien scowled, letting the balls of fire in his hands die. "Where were you when she signed her soul away to me? Father's really let heaven go to the dogs."

Jimiel scowled. "Hold your tongue, Lucifer."

Itching for a fight, Lucien stepped closer to the angel. "I have a contract with her. She belongs to me, and *only* to me, for the next three months."

Jimiel's arrogant smile made Lucifer want to rip his wings off and kick him into a never-ending abyss.

"I know the terms. You have her only on Friday night until dawn the next day. Every day between belongs to the light, to us, and I can remind her every day why she should choose our side, not the dark." Jimiel was still grinning, until Lucien smirked.

"You can be there all you like during the week, but she is still mine." Lucien knew that Jimiel couldn't reveal his true nature to Diana. It was part of the uptight rules that belonged to the good guys. Rules that Lucien didn't have to abide by. The classroom door opened, and Diana stepped out and froze when she saw Lucien and Jimiel.

Her face paled, and her gaze darted between the two men. Jimiel retrieved his bag and smiled at her.

"Ready for coffee?" he asked.

"I..." Her gaze darted between them again.

"You can go to coffee with him, or you and I can catch dinner in Paris."

"Um..." She struggled for words. "It's only noon, and I really should go with Jim. We have homework and..." Her voice grew firmer as she got braver. "I'll see you on Friday. Let's go, Jim."

"But—" Lucien sputtered, shocked. "You can't just..." But Diana was already walking away with that damned guardian angel.

"That didn't go well," Andras said.

Lucien sighed, frowning. "No," he ground out. "It certainly didn't."

"I'd be happy to smite him. I haven't fought an angel in more than two centuries. Please?" Andras asked. "Let me turn him into a pile of ash."

As much as Lucien was tempted to say yes, he knew he couldn't. Jimiel might be a little prick with wings, but he was keeping Diana safe, and Lucien didn't want anything to happen to her when he wasn't around. He felt protective of her.

Because she's mine, mine for pleasure, and I don't want my new pet destroyed. Or even damaged. It would take all the fun out of the arrangement.

"I think it's better to wait," Lucien said.

Andras let out a long-suffering sigh.

"I've been away from hell too long. Leave her to her silly angel." He opened the door that had seconds ago opened to Diana's classroom. But rather than open up to the classroom, it led to a darkened staircase. Lucien stepped through, Andras behind him as they descended into hell.

"Who was that?" Jim asked Diana as they sat down at the coffee bar just one building away from their classroom.

"He's...kind of a boyfriend?" How could she explain her situation with Lucifer to a nice, normal guy like Jim?

"How do you become a *kind of* boyfriend?" he asked, chuckling a little. The sound was sweet, nice, safe. She felt *safe* with Jim.

"I only see him on the weekends. It's a bit complicated." She sipped her mocha latte and looked away from him.

"Complicated, huh? Is he married? Sounds like what a married man wants."

Diana laughed. Lucien married? Yeah, no way. The devil didn't marry. Could he even get married? "No, he's not married." She took another sip of her coffee.

"So how do you like the class?" Jim thankfully changed the subject.

"I love it. Belkin is a great professor." She dug her notebook out to look at the homework assignment.

"So chapters four and five, then a series of questions..." She retrieved her textbook, and Jim did the same. For the next two hours, she and Jim worked on the questions.

"See you on Wednesday?" Jim asked as he took her empty coffee cup with him and threw it into the trash with his.

"Yeah, definitely." She wasn't sure why, but she suddenly had the urge to hug him. When she did, he wrapped his arms around her, and she sighed in contentment. He felt warm, not like Lucien had. He smelled nice too, like springtime. This was the kind of man a woman like her should want to be with.

"Sorry." She blushed as she let go of him.

A soft smile tugged at his lips. "You can hug me anytime, Diana. *Anytime.*"

"Er...thanks." She picked up her purse and laptop bag, still trying to ignore her red face. She really couldn't just go around hugging random guys. They'd get the wrong impression. Still...Jim was somehow different. He felt safe. The very opposite of Lucien. At least she could ignore him the rest of the week. When he'd shown up outside her classroom she'd panicked, but he hadn't been able to force her to do anything —at least he couldn't until Friday.

I'm my own woman until then. She waved goodbye to Jim and headed home. When she got back to her apartment, she found another note. Shuddering, she picked up the letter off the floor and broke the red wax seal.

Diana,

I did not find this afternoon's rebuff cute. You belong to me. Do not forget what is at stake. You are mine. Even when you are not with me during the week, the rule still applies. I do not share my toys. Ever. Stay clear of other men during our time together, or you will find an accident will befall those fools you give your favors to.

Lucien

"Give my favors to?" she growled. "It was just coffee and talking about homework!" She wasn't sure why she shouted that in her apartment all alone, but she swore she heard a chuckle.

I'm going insane, really insane.

"The devil is a dick," she muttered. Again, she heard an eerie bodiless chuckle all around her. Seth was perched on the coffee table, watching her talk to herself, his ears flattened, but he didn't hiss. That was a relief. Seth had sort of a devil radar that she found comforting.

"It's too bad I can't take you with me on Friday. I bet Lucien isn't a cat person. He is probably the kind of guy to own a snake." She snickered. Making fun of the devil did make her feel a little better. Seth's tail twitched, brushing the surface of the coffee table like a feather duster. When she flopped down on her couch, he leapt onto her and kneaded her stomach before settling down to purr.

"Save me, Seth, save me from the devil." This time she and the devil laughed together. Hers was the laugh of someone in deep despair, and his was one of victory.

There was nothing that Seth could do to save her from the devil.

❧ 8 ❧

TASTE THIS, AND BE HENCEFORTH AMONG
THE GODS. - JOHN MILTON, PARADISE LOST

T *he second Friday night*

DIANA EYED THE BLACK BOX WITH A RED SATIN BOW ON
the top as she sat in the black sedan. Lucien's driver had
opened the door for her when she'd come down to the car,
and he'd handed her the box. The letter said not to open the
box until she was instructed to. So she wore jeans, a navy-blue
sweater, and Converse shoes, and she had no intention of
changing unless Lucien ordered her to. She would likely be
ordered to strip again. The driver stopped outside the club
and helped her out. She carried her bag and the black box
inside, riding the elevator up to Lucien's suite on her own.

The doors opened to Lucien's apartment. It was empty, no
sign of her would-be seducer. She set down the bag of clothes
and books and wandered over to the bed, touching the red
velvet throw. It was the same one he'd covered her with the
last time. She almost smiled at the memory of him showing a

tiny bit of, well, humanity. She turned her attention to the feather in the glass case, unable to resist walking up to it again. The grandfather clock in the corner close by chimed away twelve times.

The feather still hung in the air, the white strands sparkling as though diamond dust had been cast over it. She wondered what Lucien would look like with hundreds of feathers like this one forming two snowy-white wings. She imagined him in the sun, wings spread wide, shimmering. He would be the most beautiful thing she'd ever seen. She was so lost in a daze that she jumped when a hand gripped her wrist, preventing her from lifting the glass. She hadn't even been aware that she was going to do that.

"I know it is tempting, but you must resist." Lucien's voice was quiet, soft.

She dropped her hand from the glass the moment he released her wrist.

"I'm sorry, it's just so beautiful, I can't..." She gave her head a little shake, trying to clear the strange fog.

"Come, we have midnight dinner reservations." Lucien slid an arm around her waist and gently pulled her away from the feather in the glass case.

"Do I need to change or—"

"Not yet. Bring your box." He let go of her to walk to the closet door and opened it. She was slowly getting used to the crazy idea that a closet door could open up to somewhere else, like a Malibu beach house. This time it was a villa in a tropical paradise.

"Where are we going?" She picked up her overnight bag and her black box and stared at the hand he held out to her. She tucked the box under her arm and placed her hand in his. He stepped through the doorway, and a humid ocean breeze lifted her hair.

Lucien grinned as he led her down the garden path illuminated by hanging colored lamps. Palm trees lined the walk-way, and when they turned, a dark band of trees opened up to reveal a building. The massive villa had golden lights all around it with an infinity pool overlooking the ocean.

"Welcome to Belize." Lucien took the box and escorted her to the villa's main glass doors. All the lights were on inside, and she could see the expensive furniture, the gleaming walnut dining room table, the dark granite kitchen, and a massive whiskey-colored couch and huge TV. The second floor probably had bedrooms. It was stunning.

"Who owns this place?"

"Me." Lucien opened one of the glass doors and allowed her to enter ahead of him.

"Why did I even bother asking?" she muttered. Lucien set the box on the coffee table by the couch and led her into the kitchen.

"No five-star chef?" she asked.

"No, tonight it's just me." He went straight to the bar. "Drink?" He opened a cabinet next to the stainless-steel fridge.

"Er...I guess. What do you have?" She glanced around at the art on the walls, which were all paintings of stormy seas. It was beautiful.

"Anything you want."

"A Bay Breeze?" she asked.

"What the hell is a Bay Breeze?" he asked, crossing his arms over his chest.

"A splash of rum, pineapple juice, and cranberry juice." She sat down on a barstool, watching Lucien as he removed his coat and rolled up the sleeves of his shirt. In that moment it all felt so normal, so like a real date. He wasn't acting like the man who'd had his hand up her skirt at the previous dinner, or the man who'd demanded she strip down to her bra and panties and lie back on his bed while he played with her.

But she could see by the fires barely banked in his eyes that it would happen again tonight. He would remind her that he owned her body and soul. Diana swallowed and glanced away from him.

"One Bay Breeze coming up." He prepared her glass, then popped a little colorful umbrella into it. She stared at the umbrella. So the devil had a sense of humor when it came to mixed drinks? She picked up her glass and took a sip. It tasted perfect, of course.

He poured himself a glass of bourbon and took a sip, then went over to the oven and he pulled the oven door down. A wave of delicious aromas traveled through the kitchen.

"Jerk chicken and hush puppies," Lucien announced as he removed two dishes and placed them on the stovetop to cool down. "I had to deep fry the hush puppies but I kept them warm in the oven."

"So the devil knows how to cook?"

"Yes, I do." He shot her smug look that shouldn't have been sexy but it was. "They have the phrase *Hell's Kitchen* for a reason. I have watched every season of *Top Chef*, by the way. Now, why do you keep doing that?" He turned to face her, retaining his relative affability, but his eyes hardened.

"Doing what?" She blinked, baffled.

"Saying *the devil* this, *the devil* that. Why?" His direct look was accusing and cold now.

"Why? Because it's true, you are the devil. So..."

He picked up his glass of bourbon and took a slow drink. "You're trying to keep your distance, reminding yourself I'm the bad guy. It's not going to work." Lucien turned back to the food and retrieved two plates and prepared their dinner.

She frowned at him. "You are the bad guy, and I won't ever forget it."

His gaze burned clear through her. "I don't want you to forget it. I want you to revel in it. I want you to bathe in darkness with me, glorify in the pleasures we share, and give yourself over to me." He raised the glass to his lips again and took another drink. She focused on the way his throat worked as he swallowed, and her skin flushed with heat. How many dreams had she had where he poured amber liquid over her bare breasts and licked them clean? Or how he'd dripped honey between her thighs and tasted her over and over.

Stop it...stop thinking about the dreams. You didn't really do those things with him. He's just getting into your head.

"Here."

He gave her a plate, and they left the kitchen. Lucien didn't stop at the dining room. He kept going. Diana followed him back to the pool, and still he didn't stop. He headed straight toward the beach, where there was a wooden hut on stilts in the ocean. They walked down to the wooden walkway over the water and into the hut.

Diana's jaw dropped. There was a massive glass floor that was lit up by an underwater light. Brightly colored fish swam below, darting through the crystal-clear water. Two cushy beanbags were on the floor nestled in the corner of the room opposite the large bed. Diana could only imagine the number of women who'd been here with him, who'd slept in his bed.

"This must be a popular place," she said, eyeing the bed. His gaze followed hers to the bed. What would it be like to lie beneath him in that bed, seeing light off the water rippling along the walls while he fucked her slow and hard? It would be... Her throat ran dry as she tried to banish the erotic images darting through her like the colorful fish in the waters below.

"The villa, yes, but not this place. I come here when I need to be alone. The water and the fish—it calms me." Lucien's admission surprised her. She turned to face him, and she didn't back away when he was right beside her. The heat of his body felt good against hers as they both watched the aquatic life. It was almost romantic...but that was insane. She focused on what he'd said and tried to stick to their conversation, even though she knew she was only delaying the inevitable.

"So, Mr. Star...do you get lonely?" She couldn't deny she was fascinated by the thought.

"I..." Lucien hesitated and then answered with a rueful smile. "I suppose I do. Hell is not a pleasant place, after all."

Diana sat down opposite him in one of the cushy black beanbag chairs and tasted her chicken. Okay, the devil could totally cook.

"What is hell like?" she asked between bites.

"You really want to know?" He raised one brow.

"Yeah, I do." She was curious. Who wouldn't be? But she also wanted to know more about his world, because it would help her understand him.

"Hell is...dark, and I don't mean that literally." Lucien stretched his legs out and crossed them at the ankles in a relaxed position while he balanced his plate on his thighs to eat.

"Dark?"

"It's tough to put into words, but it's like Dante's *Inferno*. Dante almost had it right. There aren't levels, but rather sections for specific types of sinners. You know, tyrants here, serial killers there, car salesmen on the right, mean girls from high school on the left."

"Mean girls?" Diana had seen her fair share of those.

"All those girls who were total bitches? Yeah, unless they've made a change of heart—" He mimed a plane crashing and burning with one hand and chuckled. "Lots of mean girls down there. Hate having to pass through that area, all those bitchy women. They even dare to insult me! I'm the fucking devil!"

"Wow." Diana thought back to the girl who'd bullied her

in high school. Kristina. She'd been friends with her, but the next thing she knew Kristina had played the victim on something, and everyone was on her side, calling Diana a selfish bitch. That last year of high school, she'd lost all her friends. It had been terribly lonely.

It's why you don't have friends now either. She'd kept to herself in most of her classes just to avoid drama and getting hurt.

"So..." She sipped her Bay Breeze, thinking over what she wanted to ask. "Are there really demons, heaven and hell, God and you? It's all real?"

Lucien nodded. The light from the underwater lamps illuminated his face with ripples of pale-green light.

"God is real, but he's been...absent. Not picking up the phone, if you know what I mean. His disappointment in his creations has made him withdrawn. You humans really did a number on him. Your greed, jealousy, lust, hate...all that free will made you monsters."

Diana's throat tightened. "But I thought you were the evil in the world."

Lucien snorted. "No. Evil exists out in the universe, yes, but I didn't put it there. My duty is to punish those who give in to it. The sins of humanity fall at their own feet. I merely collect the souls who need to pay the price."

"You're not really evil?" Diana struggled to wrap her mind around that.

"Not in the traditional sense. No horns, tail, or pitchfork. I can promise you that. But I'm not *good* either. When an archangel goes dark, their wings are ripped from them during the fall. One's wings are full of *grace*. Without that part of oneself, it's hard to remember how to be good. In fact, it's almost impossible."

"Wait, what's grace? Like the grace of God kind of grace?" She finished her meal and set the plate aside. Lucien did the same and reached out and placed his palm on the glass floor. Suddenly hundreds of fish were gathered in the water below, dancing in the light from the lamps. Lucien's lips curved into a smile, but it wasn't a cold or cruel one, it was softer. Her heart flipped as she saw for an instant the archangel he'd once been in that smile.

"Grace is a purity of purpose, holiness, peace, and unity with everything around you. When you lose your grace, you feel an invisible weight pressing down on you, a hollowness. Each angel describes it differently. For me it's like an ache, one so deep, so embedded inside me it will never be eased." He moved his hand on the glass and the fish responded, trailing behind him. Diana tilted back her Bay Breeze, finishing it before she slipped off the chair and knelt on the glass beside him. She placed one palm on the glass beside his, their pinky fingers almost touching.

"They like you," she noted. "My cat definitely doesn't."

"You sound surprised." Lucien chuckled. The sound was rich and dark. It sent delicious shivers down her spine.

"In the movies animals always seem to sense evil, but you aren't...not in the traditional sense." She couldn't quite explain what she was trying to say.

Lucien moved his hand, lifting it so he could trail a fingertip over the back of hers. She didn't pull away. It felt nice, and little flares of heat built in her belly at that seductive little caress.

"Most animals like me, except for dogs. They're too loyal to humans. Cats, though..." He grinned as she glanced his way. "Cats make up their own minds. Some like me fine, while others despise me. Unless I'm in a devil rage and wreaking havoc in nature, which I don't do much if at all, most animals usually don't mind me. They know on an instinctive level that I have no stake in their survival. I don't despise them the way I do humans."

She didn't address the comment about him despising humans. "You have a truce with animals?"

"Yes, that's a good way to put it."

He continued to caress her hand. She let him. Diana knew she didn't have much of a choice, and another part of her liked it like far too much. Whenever he touched her, that dark little whisper in the back of her head seemed to get louder.

"Did you get enough to eat? I confess I don't know much about mortal physiology."

"Yes, it was perfect. Thank you."

"Good." He stood and held out a hand to her. "I think it's time you explore the contents of your box tonight." She accepted his hand, and he led her from the hut. But her heart was pounding hard now, and her blood roared in her ears. The *inevitable* had arrived.

"What about the dishes? We—"

Lucien snapped his fingers, and the dishes on the tiki hut's floor vanished.

"Well that's convenient." So much for using the dishes to slow him down a bit.

He smiled at her, and this time the expression was the wicked one she was used to.

"*The devil* doesn't do dishes," he replied airily, but his lips twitched.

"Ha ha," she replied sarcastically, but she couldn't deny that tonight had been amazing so far. This place, this paradise was like something out of an expensive travel magazine. Each time she came to him, he continued to surprise her. And he wasn't scaring her, not like he had the first night. She could almost forget who he really was. *Almost.*

When they got back to the villa, he handed her the box and she opened it, her hands trembling a little. Inside was a red bikini. It looked more like a collection of straps than an actual bathing suit.

"I..." She swallowed hard and glanced at Lucien. How the hell was she supposed to put this thing on? Where did her butt go versus her breasts?

"Does this come with an instruction manual?" she asked, frowning. Maybe he'd snap his fingers and give her a more sensible suit.

"You're a smart girl—you can figure it out. Or else I imagine I'll be seeing more of you than the suit intends."

His dark eyes were no longer sweet, nor was he smiling.

"I'll grab some towels. Meet me at the pool in a few minutes." He turned and walked away.

"Okay." She exhaled slowly, removed the swimsuit from the box, and located a bathroom on the first floor. She slipped on the suit, wincing at her curvy figure in the revealing suit. Her breasts felt as if they would pop out of the tiny cups that held them. And her ass was basically falling out of the cheeky-style bottoms.

She exited the bathroom, padding toward the door that led to the pool deck. She crossed her arms over her body protectively when she went outside.

The night air was humid, and crickets hummed in the foliage of the elaborate garden beds. The heavy aroma of gardenias clung to her, but she found she liked it. The white blooms lining the path to the pool seemed to almost glow beneath the moonlight. Diana froze when she reached the pool. Moments ago the pool had been clear, but now there were dozens of floating candles lazily drifting along the top.

Lucien stood by the deep end of the pool, wearing nothing but a pair of black trunks. His bare chest was sculpted to perfection, with broad shoulders tapering to a trim waist. She couldn't help but admire the real beauty of his body. He suddenly dove into the deep end, barely making any splash as he knifed through the water. She leaned over the pool's edge, watching his body glide beneath the surface. And that's when she saw two jagged scars running just along the edges of his shoulder blades.

"When an archangel goes dark, their wings are ripped from them during the fall."

She clenched her arms tighter around herself as she imagined the agony he must have felt. Those scars had to be the remnants of the most horrific pain someone could go through. Just looking at Lucien's back made her hurt with sympathy.

Lucien broke the surface and swam toward her at the shallow end. He propped his elbows on the pool deck and curled one finger, inviting her to come closer.

"Let's see." He twirled his finger around, indicating she should spin. She did so, and her face was flushed as she faced him again.

"You look utterly fuckable," he said softly.

For a second, she dared not breathe. Then he pushed away from the side of the pool and swam a few strokes on his back. She rushed to the steps at the shallow end and hastily dropped into the warm water. She swam deeper, up to her neck so her toes touched the bottom only barely. Lucien glided in her direction. His dark hair was slicked back, and droplets clung to his long dark lashes. He stopped a few inches away from her, his body taller as he stood rather than treading water.

"Are you afraid, Diana?" he asked quietly.

Nerves skittered through her like little electric shocks as she gazed up at him. She was afraid, and yet she wasn't. The animal magnetism that drew her to him was something she wished she could ignore, but she couldn't. And that attraction overrode most of the cloying fear inside her.

"I'm afraid...afraid that I want you," she admitted.

"And you don't want to."

"Of course not. You're...a bad guy. *The* bad guy."

"I certainly am," he said, and then his voice turned husky. "But right now I'm *your* bad guy, one who wants to do every bad thing to you that you desire." He reached up to caress her bare shoulder. Diana's pulse quickened with forbidden longing.

There was a growing desire between them, but she knew it was only a matter of time before the glow became a bonfire of lust, burning them.

"I want you to say it, say that you want me." He cupped her chin, and she tilted her head back, expecting him to simply take her mouth with his, but he kept his mouth inches from hers.

"I..." She struggled to breathe. Being close to him like this made it hard to resist him. Her body wanted his, there was no denying it. But her heart and mind tried to remember who he was. She gazed into his eyes, and beyond the dark hunger she saw a glimmer of something else...*loneliness*. An ache for purity of purpose he no longer had. That ache called to her. She felt her own ache, a sense that she was missing something. She'd never known what it was, but when she looked at him, when he touched her, that ache eased.

In that moment she knew that this burning intensity between them was irresistible.

Why fight what you want? that little voice murmured in her head.

"I want you," she breathed.

Lucien brushed the pad of his thumb over her lips. "Are you sure? Once you mean it, I won't hold back."

"I mean it." She met his gaze firmly.

Her lips parted, and he licked them before he wound one arm around her waist under the water and closed the distance between them. When he took her mouth, it was slow, heated, open-mouthed, and raw. He kissed like he was fucking her mouth with his tongue, and her entire body throbbed with need. She wanted to feel him inside her.

His gentle, coaxing kiss turned sharp and wild with need. He lifted her against his body, moving through the water until he reached the steps at the shallow end. When he set her down, she parted her thighs so she could wrap her legs around his hips. She rubbed herself on his erection, which tented his swim trunks. He cupped her ass, digging his fingers hard into her. She whimpered and swallowed the sound of his kiss. When their mouths briefly broke apart, he was panting.

"I want to bend you over and fuck you," he growled. "Ram my dick inside you and pound into your ass." He growled as she arched her back, pressing tighter to him. The filthy image he painted set her traitorous body on fire. Wetness filled her, and she clenched her thighs tighter around his hips.

"You like that?" His kiss turned possessively greedy for more.

She gave in, opening her mouth to allow him to penetrate her lips with his tongue. Diana gripped his shoulders, digging in her nails, uncaring as she left scratches.

"I..." She panted, struggled to speak. "I think I want that too." She couldn't get it out of her head, the idea of him fucking her from behind, him completely in control. She'd only had missionary sex with her past boyfriends because she'd never felt comfortable asking for something more...wicked.

Lucien's merciless mouth rained hungry kisses upon her, and she didn't want to stop. When he released her, she protested with a frustrated growl, but then she was being turned around on the steps, her back facing him, and before she could even think, he was jerking her bottoms down to her knees. Then he pressed an unyielding hand on her neck, forcing her to brace on the poolside, bent over, her knees resting on the top step. The head of his thick shaft rubbed along the seam of her opening, and she moaned low as he pushed inside.

"Tight," he ground out, pushing deeper. "Fuck, you're so tight."

When he thrust all the way in, she gasped for breath. He filled every inch of her. There was no space between them, no end, no beginning. Then he started to move, slow and hard, pressing into her and then pulling out. Her arm scraped on the rough pool deck as she tried to keep from jerking forward each time his hips smacked into her ass. Normally she needed her clit stimulated, but being fucked like this turned her on just as much.

"That's it," he urged. "Take it all in, babe. Let me hear you moan," Lucien ordered.

She bit her lip to keep from making a noise. The moment she let out a panting breath, she tried to widen her legs. He had his legs on either side of hers, caging her in as he halfway leaned over her, still gripping her neck.

"You belong to me now. There's no going back." His warning came through a haze of fiery sensations, and her body rushed toward a climax. When she came, it felt like she died. Her breath ceased, every atom in her body seemed to freeze in place, and her mind blanked.

Falling...wind whipped around her. Pain sliced her back. Feathers all around her, my feathers... Gone forever. The glittering spires of the city of heaven vanished as the veil between heaven and earth was ripped open and she crashed to the ground...

❧ 9 ❧

FLOWERS OF ALL HUE, AND WITHOUT THORN
THE ROSE. - JOHN MILTON, PARADISE LOST

L ucien immediately knew something was wrong. One minute Diana was panting and writhing beneath him, and the next she crumpled into the pool.

"Diana!" He pulled out of her and lifted her up in his arms. She was limp, her face pale. Her chest rose and fell, but he couldn't seem to wake her. He cursed and closed his eyes. Seconds later they were in the hut on the water, she was naked on the bed and dry, and he was too. He turned down the blankets and tucked her into the bed. Then he laid her head on one of the pillows and brushed her hair back from her face.

What the hell had happened? He had slept with countless human females, and none of them had ever collapsed like that on him before.

"Diana," he murmured more gently as he tucked her deeper under the fluffy white comforter of the bed. She didn't stir. He sighed heavily, pressed his hand to her cheek, and closed his eyes. Flashes filled his mind—feathers, wind, the vanishing lights of heaven.

How did she see my past? My memories?

Lucien's eyes flew open, and he stared at Diana. Had she glimpsed part of his fall? No one should be able to see inside his head, no one but...Father. He was torn between wanting to recoil from her and wanting to hold her closer. Finally he surrendered to the need to have her closer and climbed into bed with her. After he wrapped his arms around her, he was calm enough to breathe.

"Diana, what are you doing to me?" he breathed. Lucien tilted his head, and then he leaned down and feathered his mouth over hers in a brushing kiss. He froze when she stirred. Her lashes fluttered, and she looked up at him.

"What...happened? I thought we were in the pool and—" She glanced around them and then down at their bodies cuddled close in the bed.

"You...fainted," Lucien said, frowning.

"I'm sorry. I don't think I've ever fainted after sex." Her nose wrinkled, and he was surprised by how adorable it was.

I'm the devil. I should not find anything a woman does adorable. Yet he did find Diana adorable. She was delicious, adorable, and fuckable. Normally he liked his bed partners to be wild-cats, with hissing cries, claws raking down his back, and heartless cold eyes staring into his. Diana was soft, warm, and all too full of light.

I'm the devil. I'm the one who is supposed to be temptation personified. Yet she is the one tempting me...back to the light.

Oh, how I have missed the taste of light and innocence.

"Are we leaving now that we've had sex?" she asked.

There was a faint vulnerability in her question that intrigued him. She thought he would take her home after this? With another woman he might, but not her.

Lucien studied her face in the dim light, watching the rippling patterns from the illuminated water below.

"Dawn is still hours away. We can stay here if you wish."

If you wish... Had he ever uttered those words to anyone?

"I like it here," she admitted. She shifted beside him and gasped. "Where's my swimsuit?"

He chuckled. "Gone. I brought you here the moment you passed out."

"I can't sleep naked," she whispered.

"Yes you can. Everyone does it."

"I don't." She lifted her chin, but the act of defiance only made him laugh. He gave her throat a playful nibble, and she wriggled beneath him in pleasure.

"Close your eyes, then, and go to sleep," he commanded, but his tone was teasing.

"I can't just go to sleep," she scoffed. "I'm lying in bed with you naked."

He slid one hand down between their bodies, then cupped her mound. She jolted as he slid one finger into her.

"Why don't I fuck you again and wear you out? You can't fight sleep if you're too tired." He thrust his finger deeper, seeking the spot that made her arch.

"Ahh!" She whimpered when he found her G spot. He worked it harder, faster, until she shuddered and her walls clamped around his digit. The climax was swift but strong, and she relaxed, panting. Even he was impressed.

"Wow." Diana suddenly yawned and snuggled deeper into the blankets. She didn't even seem to notice when he pulled his hand from between her legs. He licked his fingers, tasting her sweet juices and loving the flavor. But her eyes were already closing, and she didn't see how much he enjoyed getting her off and tasting her.

"Another time," he said. There were still three hours until dawn, and he couldn't leave her. Well, he could—but he *wouldn't*.

Lucien pulled the blankets up around their bodies and watched the light ripple over the wooden ceiling until his own eyes closed and he drifted off to sleep with Diana in his arms.

Dreams full of seaside picnics, birthday cakes, and smiling faces haunted him with their mortal lightheartedness, chasing him into darkness with their sweet light.

"Lucien." Andras's voice jerked Lucien awake just as dawn was capping the horizon. The window of the hut was glowing with the golden light. Andras stepped into view as Lucien blinked drowsily.

"What is it?"

"You're needed back in hell."

Lucien growled. He didn't want to move from this bed. Feeling the warmth of Diana's body against his own was too enjoyable. The last thing he wanted to do was go into the cold depths of hell. Everyone assumed that hell was all fire and brimstone. But most of hell was cold and dark.

"What's happening, Andras? I'm not moving until I'm certain it's worth my trouble."

"It's the housewives. They're causing trouble again."

"You're joking. Please tell me you're joking. If I have to listen to one more of those women demanding a glass of pinot grigio..." Lucien growled, his eyes blazing red. He hated those damn selfish women.

"Give me a few minutes," he finally said. Andras nodded and vanished.

Lucien looked down at Diana where she slept peacefully. He wanted to stay here with her in this small bit of paradise, but he couldn't. The levels of hell, not just the gates, needed to be tended or else all hell would break loose—literally.

With a low growl of irritation, he slipped out of the bed and snapped his fingers. Clothes manifested on his body. With another snap, he stared through a doorway to his apartment in Chicago. He wrapped his little mortal up, still asleep in a bedsheet, and carried her through the portal into his bedroom. He settled Diana onto the bed, and she curled into a ball, murmuring something. He retrieved two more blankets and layered them over her. He glanced around, noting the partially open curtains.

Dawn was here, but she could stay here as long as she liked. Normally he wanted women he slept with out of his room right away, but with Diana, he admitted he liked having her here. She belonged to him. It was only natural he kept his possession close to him, wasn't it? He wasn't getting soft, and he damned sure wasn't losing his edge. He was still the biggest badass there was. He just liked having his pet nearby, that was all.

Lucien glanced toward the feather still floating in the glass case, hoping she wouldn't touch it. His skin prickled, and the scars between his shoulder blades ached, longing for the wings he'd lost.

No. I'm not that creature anymore. Father made sure of that when he let my brother Michael tear the wings from my back.

He closed his eyes, reliving the sensations of flying from millennia ago. He could still feel the wind whipping around him and the chilly condensation of the clouds as he used to break through the tears in the dimensions between heaven and earth. The missing wings were like phantom limbs. He swore he could still feel them, but he knew that was just his body's imagination.

Diana stirred a little on the bed, turning on her side to face him. One hand stretched along the empty bed as though she searched for him. His lips twitched. He was irresistible to all women, and even quite a few men. The hunger for dark pleasure had no real limits, not when it came to craving the devil. He was like catnip to mortals. When you lived in the light, you always craved the taste of the dark, and sleeping with the devil was as dark as one could get.

"Sir?" Andras appeared in a doorway that hadn't been there seconds before.

"I'm coming." He chanced one last look at Diana before he stepped into the darkness, following Andras.

ॐ

DIANA AWOKE IN LUCIEN'S BED, LESS SURPRISED THAN THE last time to find herself there. When she moved, she winced. Her forearms were scratched from bending over on the pool deck while Lucien fucked her. Holy shit, she had slept with him, and it had been amazing.

God, I'm going to need some serious therapy. I had sex with the devil, and I liked it.

She pulled back the covers and winced as she realized she was completely naked.

"My bag!" She cursed. Had Lucien forgotten it at the villa in Belize?

"Lucien, I need my bag," she shouted. Could he hear her from wherever he was? Surely he could.

Pop! She jumped as her duffel bag appeared on the floor by the bed.

"Thanks," she said to the air, feeling that she was talking to herself.

I'll just add it as one more thing to talk to my therapist about.

Diana slid out of the bed, grabbed her bag, and headed for the bathroom. Lucien was gone, and she'd already given in to him, so part of her didn't care if he saw her naked now. She ignored the twinge of guilt over the fact that she'd really enjoyed last night. He'd gotten her to surrender to her own base desires, ones that would keep her blushing for days if she ever had to tell anyone about them. And the worst part was, he'd been right. Sex with him was out of this world.

She eyed the massive shower at the end of the bathroom

and suddenly grinned. Oh yeah, she was totally going to shower here. The shower was a beautiful black marble structure surrounded on two sides by glass. A big white marble bench sat in the corner, and rotating showerheads were built into the front of the shower. Diana turned on the spray and waited until the steam cocooned her before she climbed in. The hot water singed her skin deliciously, and she sighed. As she washed, she touched herself carefully. She was sore between her thighs, but it didn't feel bad. She been truly fucked and fucked hard, but it had been *so good*. She couldn't resist exploring herself, slipping a finger inside. Her body trembled at the penetration. She'd never done that before, and she couldn't deny the new changes inside her made her want to explore her sensuality in ways she never had until today.

"Now that is a welcome sight."

She gasped and spun around at the sound of Lucien's voice. He stood just outside the glass, watching her.

"Oh please, don't stop. I'm quite content to watch." He put one palm on the glass and leaned in, as though to get a better look.

Shame and embarrassment rippled through her. She shouldn't have been doing *this* where he could see her.

"I..." The words died upon her tongue as she noticed that his pupils were slightly red. Was he mad or—

"Please, darling, touch yourself. Give me what I *want*," he said. "Let me see you climax by stroking that little bundle of nerves. But if you're too scared or embarrassed, I'd be happy to join you. I'm sure I can give you what you need."

Her nipples tightened, and an ache tugged low, sending ripples of excitement through her body. "I know," she said breathlessly.

She shivered with longing. She wanted his cock inside her, stretching her and filling her almost to the point of pain. Yes, that was what she wanted. She couldn't admit that to him, because it felt like giving in to him, surrendering, and that felt wrong...even when she'd signed a contract to do just that, obeying his commands and yielding to her secret, hidden sexual desires.

His eyes softened, and the eerie red glow subsided as he seemed to read her thoughts.

"I could take you...if you didn't say no." There it was, the dark offer she needed. If she said no, he would stop, but he would take her if she didn't say no. She backed up in the shower, her palms flattening against the wall behind her as he slowly began to undress. By the time he was down to just a pair of black briefs, her body hummed. She hadn't forgotten the pool, how it had felt to be owned by him. It had felt wrong, and yet part of her felt free.

Lucien opened the shower door and stepped inside, now completely naked. It was her first chance to really see him. He was chiseled perfection, each muscle defined and sculpted, but he didn't really look like a bodybuilder. His body was that of a warrior, honed and hard-edged. And his hands...they were elegant yet not weak. His long fingers were designed perfectly to touch her and make her burn with desire.

He really had been an angel. No one could have been that perfect.

"No turning back now, darling," he whispered as he closed the shower door and reached for her.

His hands gripped her hips, jerking her against him, demanding that she submit. His body branded hers with heat as he pressed her back against the wall.

"Do you like the idea of me fucking you without asking for permission?" he whispered against her ear. "Knowing that I'll just take what I want because I own this little body?" He smoothed his hands down over her breasts, cupping them before he gave each nipple a sharp tug.

"Answer me," he demanded, fisting his hand in her hair and pulling so there was just a hint of pain, a pain that made her body explode with life.

"Yes!" she shouted, her cry bouncing off the shower walls.

"Yes, what?" He gave her hair another tug, and he slipped his other hand between her thighs to find her clit. He pressed his fingertip down hard on it, the pressure too much for her sensitive bud. She jerked in his hold, trying to escape the onslaught of pleasure.

"I want you to fuck with me without asking," Diana panted.

"Good girl," he praised before he nipped her ear with his teeth in a playful bite. She wanted to hate his condescending words, but she didn't. They made her hotter. She wanted to be that good little girl who pleased him, who gave herself over to him in every way and received intense pleasure in return.

She whimpered as he gave one ass cheek a harsh slap, then sighed as he rubbed the sting away with gentle strokes. He covered her trembling body with his own as he claimed her mouth with his. Lucien gripped one of her legs, jerking her thigh up so her leg curled around his hip. Then he lifted her other leg up. She sucked in a sharp breath as his cock impaled her while he pinned her to the shower wall. The marble seared her skin from the heat of the water, and she lost herself in his seductive taste. His cock filled her, blocking out all thoughts and leaving only primal need. She clawed at his back as he fucked her slow and hard against the shower wall. The more they kissed, the more her control, her thoughts, her very breath seemed to slip away...away into him. Only one thought broke through the rush of darkness. Could the devil consume her soul?

Light...sweet light...feathers gone...pain too much...wind...

Diana struggled to breathe as the darkness closed in, but she heard his voice.

"Stay with me. Don't look away."

Her eyes opened, and she focused on Lucien's dark eyes. His pupils held only a hint of a frightening crimson hue. He gripped her ass, holding her up as he continued to fuck her, and the rubbing of his body on her clit and his thick shaft filling her were too much. Her body exploded with invisible fire, and her senses shattered as she came. She was dimly aware of him ramming into her over and over, jackhammering toward a desperate climax. For long seconds, they remained fused together, bodies dripping wet from sweat and the water still running down.

"Fuck." Lucien buried his face against her neck. His body trembled as he slowly let her go, and she landed on shaky legs. She used the shower wall for much-needed support as she caught her breath. She couldn't shake the images or sensations of what she'd experienced when she kissed him, that sense of falling from grace and the unbearable agony and pain at losing her wings...*his* wings. It was his memory, not hers, yet she felt it as though it had been her own.

Lucien jerked the shower nozzle toward his chest, covering himself in the spray, and then after a second he glanced her way, his black gaze unreadable. Suddenly he vanished.

"Are you kidding me?" She groaned and shoved her face beneath the shower spray and sighed. Her body still trembled with little aftershocks. He'd just fucked her and then vanished. A flush of shame rolled through her, and her eyes burned with tears, but she held them back. She finished showering, washing off his scent, the ghostly feel of his touch, everything.

I'll just try to pretend it didn't happen.

It would be impossible, but she had to try. Once all these midnights with Lucien were over, she would go back to her normal life and try to forget this. She stepped out of the shower and reached for a fluffy white towel. Steam fogged the mirror, and Diana smeared a hand over the glass so she could see herself. She looked tired, as tired as she'd felt in the last few years watching her dad's illness eat away at his life and strength.

Don't forget who you're doing this for, remember?

Diana twisted her wet hair into a braid and quickly changed into her spare clothes. The bathing suit was gone, probably back in Belize, and she was glad. She didn't want any reminders about last night. She felt cheap and ashamed. Not about what she'd done but because of *who* she'd done it with.

He'd said he wanted her innocence, so maybe if she wasn't innocent anymore he'd lose interest. That wouldn't be her fault. Nothing in the agreement said he couldn't terminate the contract if he got bored. He could just make her dad sick again, couldn't he? Or maybe not...

Diana remembered the letter from the attorney when she'd received the contract. If she could meet with him, she could get some clarification. She wasn't above playing like a bad girl to reduce her innocent appeal. And after last night, she knew she would enjoy it all too much.

The driver was waiting for her when she left Lucien's apartment, and she nodded at him. He answered with a more relaxed smile.

"I'm Diana, by the way. I feel we should be on a first-name basis after all the time we'll spend together."

The driver chuckled. "Fair enough. I'm Douglas."

"Do I call you Doug?" she asked, grinning.

"No way. I hate Doug."

"Douglas it is." She held out her hand, and the driver

shook it. Then she climbed into the back seat. Once he was behind the wheel, she spoke again.

"So how did you end up working for the devi—I mean Mr. Star?"

"Well..." He pulled out into traffic and took his time answering. "I was in a bit of trouble. My construction company went underwater—financially, I mean."

Diana settled her duffel bag over her lap and held her breath, waiting for him to continue.

"One day I'm driving out in the country. I'm feeling like shit, and I know my wife and three kids are relying on me to get the business back up and running or else we would lose our house and..." He paused again, his voice a little rougher than before.

"I was feeling bad, really bad, and I had to stop my car and get out. I was a few seconds away from jumping in front of the next truck that barreled down the road. And that's when I saw him. Mr. Star just materialized in the center of the crossroads." Douglas drummed one finger on the steering wheel.

"He comes over to me and asks me what I would do to save my company."

"What did you say?" Diana thought back to the moment in the hospital chapel when she'd told Lucien she would give anything to save her father's life.

"Anything," Douglas echoed.

"Same here," she replied softly. "My dad had colon cancer."

"Shit, I'm sorry," Douglas said. His gaze met hers in the rearview mirror.

"He's better now, obviously." She chuckled dryly. "So what's your deal? With Lucien, I mean."

"I get the pleasure of being his weekend chauffeur. Usually

he can just appear where he wants. I'm sure you've seen him do it?"

Diana nodded.

"Sometimes he likes me to just drive him around. He'll sit in the back seat and tell me to drive until the gas tank's almost empty."

"Hmmm..." Diana couldn't fathom why Lucien would want to do that.

"I guess he likes to have time to think or something," Douglas said. "It must suck to be the king of hell. Think of all the bad, irritating shit you'd have to put up with. He once told me he had to deal with Joseph Stalin. Can you imagine? I would hate that job too."

Diana sat back, a dozen thoughts beating around her head. Maybe Douglas was onto something. What if the devil didn't like his job, didn't like being evil? He'd already told her that he didn't create sin, people did, and that he didn't make people sin, he only punished them if they went astray. There were people he enticed into corruption, but he never made them corrupt. He merely offered opportunities.

"Douglas, do you know where the office of Lionel Barnaby is?"

"Mr. Star's lawyer? Yeah, why?"

"I want to ask a few questions about my contract. Do you think he's in his office on a Saturday?"

The driver chuckled. "Looking for loopholes? I did the same. Yeah he works Saturdays."

"Did you find any loopholes?" she asked hopefully.

"Nope. He drafted that thing solidly. Barnaby's office is at 7923 East Parkway Avenue."

Diana fiddled with the zipper on her duffel bag, thinking. If she could find out whether there were any loopholes, she might still be able to save her dad without any more midnight visits. After last night, she knew that if she kept going to see him, she would truly lose herself in him.

"Here we are," Douglas said as he pulled up in front of her apartment.

"Thanks." She slipped out of the car and threw her duffel bag over her shoulder. Her thoughts were miles away as she headed to her apartment. How on earth was she going to find a loophole in a deal with the devil?

❧ 10 ❧

AND SHOULD I AT YOUR HARMLESS
INNOCENCE MELT, AS I DO. - JOHN MILTON,
PARADISE LOST

Jimiel lingered outside the door to Diana's apartment, thoughts rushing through his head. He needed to find a way to protect Diana. He had been given clear orders from Michael himself.

She must live. She must be kept safe.

Jimiel had failed Diana.

From the moment she'd been born he'd been there, watching over her, keeping her safe. He'd been her imaginary friend, her school ground playmate, the boy at the prom who danced with her when her date bailed on her. Every pain he could spare her, he had. Until her father's illness. There were some things he couldn't help, not without crossing the line. Going against orders was just as bad as failing to keep her alive. So he watched, he waited. He had borne each of her pains in his own heart. Angels did not feel pain the way mortals did. When Diana cried, her heart felt like it was bleeding and cut from her chest. Yet she continued to breathe, continued to be strong. With an angel, it was different.

Jimiel placed a hand on her door, using his extra senses to

listen to her talk to her cat. He smiled a little, despite his worry. She was tough. His little mortal charge could handle almost anything.

When angels experienced pain, it affected every cell of their body. Like a pulse of electricity shooting through them, frying every fiber of their being and paralyzing them. Angels were hard to hurt and nearly impossible to kill. That made them strong enough to fight the demons. Demons were angels who had been so fully corrupted that they'd left the light behind. Jimiel rarely encountered demons. His heavenly job assignments were usually to help share the burden of a human's pain. More than once Jimiel had visited Diana's father for such a purpose.

I couldn't heal him, but no one said I couldn't ease his pain. So he had sat with the man for hours, lightly touching his hand and siphoning off the pain. It had been worth it to see Diana's face when her father had said he felt good and had no pain that day. It hadn't stopped her tears each time she returned to her car in the hospital parking lot, but it had given her some relief.

But how could he save Diana from Lucifer? The fallen angel was powerful, the king of hell itself. No normal angel could survive a battle with him. Even archangels tiptoed around him when their paths sometimes crossed. Lucifer may be the devil, but he had been known to many as the favorite son, the brightest star. Not even the blackness of the end of the world could have dimmed his burning beacon when he'd been an angel of the light.

Jimiel had never known him then, but the stories... Lucifer before the fall had been a legend. But his pride had been too strong, and his need to be more important than the humans Father created had been his undoing.

Pride goeth before the fall.

Jimiel studied the door to Diana's apartment, wondering

how he could save her from the devil. She was going to visit an attorney this morning, that much was clear. He would listen in on that conversation, just in case there was something worth hearing. If he could find a way to circumvent the time Lucifer spent around her, then he might be able to stop Lucifer from corrupting her. Every soul that Jimiel had seen make deals came out darker, hungrier for the things they shouldn't want, like pain, death, greed. So far, Diana hadn't shown any signs. A little rough sex wasn't darkness, not to angels. No, it was greed for money, greed for power, a lust for hurting others. He would do anything to stop Lucifer from turning Diana into that.

Anything.

LUCIEN PROWLED INTO THE CAVERNOUS ROOM OF HIS office in hell. It held a rather rustic, otherworldly charm that clearly screamed "the devil works here," with the black diamond fireplace, the large roughhewn dark wood desk, the chains on one wall, and a few torture implements on the other side. But he rarely spent time down here. Torture wasn't his thing. He outsourced that to the more trustworthy demons he kept imprisoned in hell. Most fallen angels like him weren't drawn to pain, either to feel it or to cause it. Angels had one weakness. Pleasure in all forms. It was an emotion that they should only experience in the presence of their father, unless they fell. They were free to taste the world as humans do, but everything was still a little faded.

Pleasure that was dimmed was still better than no pleasure at all. Andras was like him, focused on pleasure, but as the Fallen they faced the task of being the gatekeepers to hell. Angels who went too far, who loved the darkness too much, always changed. The ones who loved death, pain, greed, and power mutated into the worst demons. Lucifer had dominion over them, despite his own loathing of them.

"Everything all right?" Andras asked as he materialized in the doorway.

"Yes." The word was a lie. They both knew it. One of the funny things about hell? You couldn't hide the truth, not once you passed the gates. A lie uttered even from Lucien's lips held an easily detectable ring of falseness to it.

"It's her, isn't it? You went back to her this morning."

"I did." He had returned when he shouldn't have, but she'd called his name and had asked for her bag, and he'd wanted to see her just once more. He'd expected to see her leaving his penthouse, but she hadn't been leaving—she had been in *his* bathroom ready for a shower. He had lingered there, invisible, watching her strip naked. It hadn't been her naked body that had fascinated him, but *her*. There had been a soft, alluring vulnerability to her that called to the dead part of him, the angel he had been before the fall. Angels had been created to serve and protect, to guide. Vulnerability brought out those angelic instincts.

"Are you sure she's worth the risk?" Andras asked.

"Risk?" Lucien leaned back against the front of his desk, eyeing his friend.

Andras shrugged. "The more you bring her into your world, the more she tastes the dark, the more you will crave her light. It happens to all of us."

"Even you?" Lucien asked, curious about Andras's sudden openness. Usually the fallen angel kept his thoughts closed off and his mind clear of such concerns.

"Even me. I have been tempted once. But I stayed away. She reminded me too much of what I had once been. We can't have both worlds, the light and the dark. Only mortals are that fortunate."

Lucien crossed his arms. "I have no intention of *returning*.

You know heaven would never allow it. They stuck me with this job, and I have to see it through until the end...whenever that may be."

There was nothing more hellish than facing hundreds of millennia of this as his sole purpose. Only Diana had given him a purpose in the last few days. Being around her had rejuvenated him, giving him a feeling of light.

"Be careful, Lucien, that's all I'm saying. Don't let a mortal get a hold over you," Andras warned.

Lucien wanted to rage at the other angel, but he couldn't. Andras was right. If he wasn't careful, Diana could take him over, make him forget who he was and the power he wielded.

Fury dotted his vision with black spots. *I am the fucking king of hell. No one controls me. No one.*

He would keep playing with the little mortal, but he would not let her hold sway or gain any power over him. She was a toy—a lovely, sweet, intoxicating toy. He glanced at Andras.

"Did you have anything else to say?"

Andras's blue eyes sparked with red fire.

"The demons are restless. You need to give them work to do or they'll focus on destruction topside. I don't know about you, but I'm sick of the violence they cause."

Lucien agreed. Demons topside were a bad thing. They usually caused natural disasters and other destruction.

"I'll take care of it. You focus on the guardian angel Jimiel. I want to know what he's up to. He's guarding Diana for a reason. I want to know why. It can't be a coincidence."

"Agreed." Andras vanished, and the soft flutter of invisible shadow wings was the only evidence he'd been there seconds before.

Lucien knew he needed to stay in the realm of hell for a while longer, but once he'd seen everything was back in order, he'd go spy on his toy. The thought curled his lips into a devil-may-care-grin that only made him laugh darkly.

I may care indeed.

❧❧

DIANA SAT IN A CREAM-COLORED LEATHER CHAIR IN THE brightly lit modern lobby of the law firm of Barnaby, Denton, Riggsley, and Jones LLP. It was only ten in the morning, but she was glad the law firm was open on a Saturday. A beautiful brunette receptionist in her early twenties smiled at Diana from behind the expensive granite counter of the front desk. As the woman answered phone calls, Diana examined her surroundings. Glass offices lined the walls on either side of the lobby, and whenever a lawyer closed his or her door, the glass frosted, giving them privacy with their clients. It had to cost a fortune to have an entire floor of offices like that.

I guess working for the devil pays well.

"Miss Kingston, Mr. Barnaby will see you now. Please follow me." The receptionist slipped her headset off and got up, waiting for Diana to follow. They walked to the end of the hall, and she was shown into a corner office.

"Mr. Barnaby, this is Miss Kingston," the receptionist announced, and she closed the door, sealing them inside the frosted glass. Diana turned her focus to the man who rose from the desk and held out his hand for her to shake.

"It's a pleasure to meet you, Miss Kingston." Mr. Barnaby was in his fifties, and he was rather ordinary with slightly silver hair and kind eyes. Diana had honestly expected somebody sleazy or slimy.

"It's nice to meet you too, Mr. Barnaby." Diana shook his hand.

"Please, call me Lionel. Have a seat." He waved toward a pair of expensive armchairs that faced his desk, and she sat.

"Now," Lionel said as he smiled again. "How may I help you? You are here for the midnight contract, right?"

"The midnight contract?" Diana asked.

"Oh yes!" The attorney chuckled. "That's what my filing system has it as. Each contract with Mr. Star has a unique element to it. In your case, you meet with Mr. Star at midnight."

"Oh, right." She nodded slowly. "That makes sense."

"What questions do you have?" Lionel settled back in his chair, patient and polite.

Diana still couldn't believe she was talking to the devil's attorney. "Well..." She tried not to fidget. "It's about the termination clause. If Mr. Star gets bored with me before three months of Fridays are up, does that void the contract?" She paused, clearing her throat. "I mean, like if he decides he doesn't want me anymore, my dad's condition couldn't go back to..."

"Will your father die?" Lionel steepled his fingers and peered at her over the tips of his fingers.

"Yes." She held her breath, terrified of the answer.

"No, he won't die. Mr. Star admits that his attention can wander. Over the years I've worked as his counsel, I've been able to guide him toward a rule that contracts cannot be broken based on whims. If there is one thing he understands and supports, it's rules."

"But he's...you know...isn't he supposed to be all about breaking rules?" Diana couldn't see Lucien playing by any rules.

"From what I understand of Mr. Star's situation, he doesn't mind rules and fairness. Strange, I know, but it has to do with the cosmic balance. The light and the dark are bound by equal rules."

"My dad is safe, even if the devil—I mean Mr. Star—loses interest in me?"

"Yes. He won't break his promise," Lionel reassured her. "Did you have any other questions?"

Diana nodded. "I do." One question had been oddly burning into her mind on the way over to Lionel's office. "What happens if I miss a Friday? Not by my choice, but if something happens to keep me from coming against my will?"

"Like having an unavoidable conflict?"

"Yeah."

"You will need to reach out to Mr. Star and explain your situation. Another day may be negotiated, but there's no guarantee. I will of course be happy to speak with him on your behalf should a situation arise. I would be remiss if I didn't encourage you to see an attorney to represent you if you want the contract analyzed. Of course, that may be difficult given Mr. Star's identity and the nature of the contract. I represent Mr. Star's interests, not yours, however I do attempt fairness as much as possible. I'd be happy to speak to anyone you hire for representation."

"Thank you. I can't really afford an attorney right now. My father's medical bills wiped me and my mom out financially."

"I understand completely. Well, as I said, you may come to me at any time. Do you have any other questions?" Lionel asked.

"No, that's it I think." She stood up, and Lionel shook her hand again.

"Just call or stop by if you have any other questions."

"Thanks."

As she left the attorney's office, Diana felt for the first time that she had a chance to control the situation. If she made herself too easy, if she made him think she was no longer a challenge, he might leave her alone and look for more interesting girls to pursue. It was clear he wanted a challenge, and if she no longer was one, then he would let her father live and let her go back to her normal life and she'd...

Diana cleared her head of the thought of never seeing him again. He was the devil; she needed to pursue this loophole in their contract and go free. She couldn't allow herself to think of anything else.

She had a barbeque with her parents that afternoon but she knew she had just enough time to squeeze in a visit to Amara. She arrived on street with the Occultist's Apothecary shop around lunchtime. She parked her car and went inside. Amara was standing by the window hanging a collection of crystals connected by brightly colored strings to what looked like talismans from various cultures. The afternoon sunlight was caught in the crystals and fractured into shafts of multi-colored light that danced along the bottles of ingredients and the books that filled the shelves. The sight was spellbinding.

"Diana!" Amara greeted her warmly and set the extra crystals on a nearby table.

"Amara." Diana suddenly had the urge to hug this woman. She was the only person who understood what Diana was going through.

"Come, child." Amara chuckled and opened her arms.

Diana rushed to hug the other woman tight. She didn't mind that Amara had called her *child*. The other woman was probably only ten years older than her, but it sounded like a sweet endearment.

"You've changed," Amara murmured as they let go of each other. The beautiful black woman cupped Diana's chin and studied her face closely.

"Changed?" Diana swallowed hard. That didn't sound good at all.

"Yes. There's a glow around you."

"A glow? Not a shadow?" she asked as Amara waved her to the back of the shop.

"Let me read your leaves again." Amara poured a cup of tea, and they sat down at the table.

"What did you mean about a glow?" Diana took a long gulp of her tea. It tasted like a soft chamomile and velvet.

"A glow is like an aura, but purer. Auras reflect moods, so they are always temporary. A glow is permanent. It has to do with one's being, not one's mood."

"But...shouldn't I be shadowy or something?"

"What makes you say that?" Amara asked as she took the mostly empty cup from Diana and turned it over on its saucer to drain the last bits of the tea before she turned it back over and studied the shapes in the cup from the ground-up tea leaves.

"Well..." Diana's face flooded with heat. "He...we...hooked up last night. And this morning."

"You 'hooked up' with the devil?" Amara chuckled. Diana was amazed that Amara could laugh. She was brave enough to laugh at the devil and the darkness as though she was scared of nothing.

"I did." Diana folded her hands in her lap and stared at them.

"He didn't force you?" Amara's caramel-brown eyes were serious now, all humor gone.

"No. Definitely not. It was totally consensual." A little too much. She'd been begging him for it.

"And you're upset because you didn't want to want him?" Amara tilted her teacup, her eyes studying it once more.

"Yeah. I mean that's right, isn't it? I shouldn't want him. He's bad, like the ultimate bad boy."

"He certainly is," Amara said. She set the cup down and sighed. "But giving yourself to him, wanting him, it gave you the glow."

"What? But how is that even—" She couldn't make sense of that.

"When you desired him, what drew you in?" Amara asked.

"Well, it was just him, the way he was smiling, looking at

me. And he'd taken me to a romantic place and..." She couldn't put into words how she'd felt when they'd been close in the pool. The energy between them had been completely electric, like a broken power line falling on a road during a storm. It had been frightening and alluring, and the burn of touching it had nearly killed her, yet she was left wanting more.

"You didn't want his power—you wanted *him*. That's not the same, you see? You wanted the angel, not the devil."

"But he's not an angel anymore, is he?" she asked.

"Course he is. An angel is still an angel, merely a fallen one."

"Oh...I see." Diana watched as Amara poured her another cup of tea. "Was my first reading not okay?"

"No, it was fine. This is to calm your nerves. Chamomile will help you relax."

"Thanks." Diana drank her new cup of tea.

"Now," Amara said as she leaned back in her chair, "the tea leaves tell me that you are bound to the dark, but not consumed by it. That is good. You must continue to listen to your instincts. Perhaps being with him is not so bad. It may be your destiny."

Diana laughed a little incredulously. "Destiny? But I don't believe in anything like that."

"Just because you don't believe doesn't mean something isn't true." Amara's serious reply made Diana's heart flutter. She hadn't believed in the devil or even hell—at least she wasn't sure if she did or not. Yet Lucien had proven he existed, contrary to her beliefs.

"So you're saying I should totally give in to the devil and enjoy the ride?"

Amara's eyes were warm with silent laughter.

"No, no, of course not. Merely listen to yourself, protect yourself, but if something feels right to you, even if society's rules tell you it might be wrong, trust yourself first. That's all I'm saying."

"Ahh." She took another sip of the velvety tea. A quiet silence settled between them that neither of them seemed quick to break. "Thank you for being here for me. I don't have anyone else I can talk to about this, you know."

Amara reached across the table and squeezed her hand. "Destiny brought you to my door, and I won't turn you away."

"Thanks." Diana finished her tea and picked up her coat and purse. Her cell phone buzzed, and she checked the messages.

Unknown number: Even your tea leaves are right. You belong to me.

Lucien. There was only one person who could know about her and Amara meeting.

"It's him," Amara said, though she was seven feet away and couldn't see the screen.

"The devil has my phone number. Ugh." Diana groaned. "And he's spying on me," she announced loudly. "Which is the opposite of cool, by the way." She knew he could hear her. Amara raised a questioning brow.

"Sorry, I know I look crazy, but he can hear me when I talk," she explained. Her phone buzzed again, and she looked at the screen.

Unknown number: I'm not cool, I'm hot. Haven't you figured out that by now? ;-)

He finished the text with a pineapple emoji.

What the hell did the pineapple emoji mean? She saved the number in her phone under one word as the name: *Asshat*. Now at least she could get a laugh each time he messaged or called her.

Diana: What does the pineapple mean?
Asshat: If you don't know, you'll never guess.
Diana: That was nice and cryptic.

"Are you all right to drive home?" Amara asked.

"Yeah, thanks again." She gave Amara one more hug and headed for her car. It was going to be a long week if Lucien kept texting her over and over.

Asshat: *Where you going now?*

Diana stared her phone screen as she sat in her car.

Diana: Stop texting me. I'm about to go to the grocery store, and I won't text and drive, not even for you. By the way, I hate emojis.

Asshat: *The person who created emojis has a spot reserved in my workplace. Don't worry, he'll get his comeuppance.*

Diana snorted, a little surprised he made her laugh. She put the phone on silent and tucked it into her purse before she started her car. This afternoon she had a barbecue at her parents' house with her parents' neighborhood block, and the last thing she needed was to be bothered with the devil.

❧ I I ❧

The little supermarket Diana stopped at was a high-end one that her mother liked. Armed with the list her mother had sent her, she parked her car and retrieved her purse before she exited the vehicle.

"You weren't kidding." A dark voice chuckled, and she jumped. Lucien was leaning against the side of her car.

"How the heck did you—you know what? Never mind."

Lucien chuckled. He still wore a black suit and his signature red tie. He looked so intimidating and out of place in the parking lot of the store. She couldn't help but remember how he'd used that red tie to bind her wrists while he tortured her with pleasure in his bed. Her thighs clenched and her womb throbbed to life at the memory. She'd never look at red ties the same way again.

"I don't even have to read your thoughts," he murmured silkily as he stroked his hand over the tie and then flashed her a wicked look. "I'll be sure to use it again. The next time I'll fuck you so hard you'll be hoarse from screaming."

Diana blinked, unable to speak for several seconds, and

then she shook off the erotic enchantment his words had cast over her.

"You have to stop saying things like that...at least in public."

"Noted." He glanced around. "I'll be sure to tell you *everything* I'm going to do to you once we're alone."

They stared at each other, the electricity sparking between them until a car alarm made Diana jump and Lucien's focus break. A woman nearby had hit her alarm on accident and was frantically trying to get it to stop.

Lucien rolled his eyes, and with a snap of his fingers, the alarm turned off.

"So, let's go shopping. I'm curious to see how mortals grocery shop. I never usually watch humans do much of anything unless it involves lust, money, or power." He waved to the woman walking past them pushing a cart full of food. She glanced at them, frowning.

"Maybe you should cool it on the whole *mortal* thing. If people think you're crazy, they might call the police."

Lucien flashed her a devastating grin. "Oh, don't tempt me, darling. I've got handcuff fantasies on the list for next Friday night."

A hot blush burned Diana's face, and she grabbed his arm, dragging him toward the store.

"Let's just get in there, get the stuff, and get out."

"Why in such a hurry?" he demanded, but his lips twitched.

"I have to go to a thing this afternoon, so the sooner I can satisfy your need to play the mortal, you'll leave and I can get back to my life."

"Now, hold on, you can't just shrug me off. Yes, at midnight on Friday you do have to do as I wish, but the rest of the week there is nothing stopping me from joining you as you do whatever it is you do."

They entered the store, and classical music filled the air. The soft floral scent of freshly cut flowers made Diana relax. She did love shopping here, even if it was more expensive.

"You really plan to tag along while I shop for groceries? Don't you have people to maim, torture, and bring to the dark side?"

He pushed back the sleeve of his suit and checked his expensive Cartier wristwatch. It had a red quartz face. No surprise there, she thought. The man loved black and red.

"I've got time between maiming and torture sessions."

"Oh lucky me." She couldn't help but layer the response in sarcasm.

Lucien ignored her and grabbed the nearest cart and began pushing it. The sight was almost comical, with men and women in the store watching him as he headed toward the produce section. The men looked on with envy and the women with desire.

Diana sighed and rushed to catch up.

"What is on your list?" Lucien asked as he picked up a very big pineapple and set it in the cart.

"Well, pineapples aren't." She reached for the fruit to return it to the display stand, but he smacked her hand away, tsking.

"That's for me, darling."

"What is it with you and pineapples?"

"The devil has to keep a few secrets," he said cryptically, but the glint in his eyes told her he was teasing.

She focused on her list. "Hot dogs, hamburgers, buns for both, coleslaw—"

"Good God, what sort of party is this?" He plucked the list from her hands, eyeing it.

"A barbecue." Diana tried to take the list back, but he wouldn't let her.

"You know, I've never been to one. I think I shall 'tag along,' as you put it."

"No!" she gasped. "You can't." The devil at her neighborhood barbecue was a *terrible* idea.

"Yes I can." He curled one arm around her waist and leaned in as though to kiss her cheek, but instead he whispered in her ear, "I can do *anything* I like. Never forget that." He licked the shell of her ear, and she shivered as her body awakened with desire. She nearly burned up with mortification when she noticed an older lady watching them.

"I'll get the meat. I love the butcher." Lucien left her to walk up to the counter about ten feet ahead of her. The older woman wheeled her cart up to Diana's, smiling.

"Keep a hold of that one, dear. He'll make beautiful babies."

"Thanks," Diana said. Her face was hot, so she was surprised she wasn't steaming.

She looked at Lucien's back as he leaned casually over the curved glass of the deli counter and talked to the butcher. The butcher laughed at whatever Lucien said as he collected fresh hamburger patties. A young woman pushing a stroller stopped next to Lucien while she ordered some fresh salmon. Her child, a little boy, was fussing, but he cooed and waved his arms at Lucien, who glanced down at him. For a second Diana was worried Lucien would do something to make the child cry. Lucien merely grinned at the baby, and the child squealed in delight, clapping his chubby little hands. Diana hastily walked up to stand beside Lucien on the other side.

"Thank you," the mother said as she collected her salmon and turned to Lucien. "He's been fussing all day—teething, you know. This is the first laugh he's had in days."

"He's a cute little guy." Lucien flashed another grin at the kid before he glanced at Diana. "What?"

"You made him laugh." Diana simply stared at him. How did he keep surprising her like this? Just when she thought she had him figured out, he proved he was even more unpredictable.

"I like children." He shrugged.

"You do?"

"Yes. Children are pure. They aren't complex. It's refreshing."

"Huh." So he was into pure...like her. He'd said her soul was pure.

"I am still an angel, you know. Angels love children. We share a lot in common with them. We both believe our parents are the beginning and end of our existence, and things in the world the delight us." He took charge of the cart again and leaned his elbows on the handle.

"What's next?" he asked.

"Er..." She checked her list. "Buns."

"Buns." He chuckled. "*Buns* it is."

"Stop saying that!" she hissed, but part of her wanted to laugh.

"Buns are on aisle five," he announced loudly, drawing the stares of everyone around them.

"Stop!" She giggled and jabbed one elbow into his ribs.

"Oh, you're no fun. Perhaps your buns need to be warmed," he teased and mimed a spank in the air. A woman giving away free samples of cheese nearly choked when she saw Lucien spanking the air.

Diana pushed him and the cart down the nearest aisle, which thankfully had no other shoppers in it.

"I can't take you anywhere." Diana shook her head, but despite the embarrassment she was laughing. She hadn't realized how tightly wound she had been for so long, ever since her father had gotten sick. She'd bottled up all her tears, fears, worries, and darker emotions, and now she felt them escaping. They seemed to be leaking out and evaporating like morning mist.

"You should laugh more," Lucien said softly. His dark eyes burned hers, and the heat of it made her feel a little dizzy.

"Why?" she replied.

"Because it is a beautiful sound, and...you need to. I could see that pain you bottled up. It isn't good for your soul."

She arched her brow. "You care about the good of my soul? I thought the devil liked to hurt people?"

"Actually, I do care. I want you pure and lighthearted. I have plenty of dark and angry souls to deal with at the office. I made a bargain with you because you're not like that."

Diana wasn't quite sure what to say. She cleared her throat and focused on the grocery list.

"We need chips. Some tortilla ones." She pointed to a rack, and Lucien grabbed two bags and then waited patiently for her next order.

"Um...a brownie mix for dessert."

"Mix?" He frowned. "What is a *mix*?" The way he said the word *mix* made it sound disgusting.

"It's powdered brownie mix in a box."

"Ugh. No, we aren't doing that. This way." He pushed a shopping cart to the bakery and picked up a freshly made cake and presented it to her with a cocky grin. She stared at the label and rolled her eyes.

"Devil's food cake. Why am I not surprised?"

"These are quite excellent." He set the cake in the cart, and if the devil could preen, he was certainly doing it now. "What else?" he asked.

"That's it. After the buns, I mean."

"You want me to say *buns* again, don't you?" Lucien grinned wickedly.

"No!" She laughed and grabbed several bags of buns for both hot dogs and hamburgers.

"We don't need anything else?" Lucien glanced around the store hopefully.

"You really like shopping, don't you?" She laughed at his baffled expression.

"I suppose I do." He guided the shopping cart to the nearest line. She quickly put their items on the belt for a scanner.

"You check out yourself?" Lucien watched her in fascination.

"Do you ever spend time in the world in normal places?"

"Not really." He paused and handed her items. "I stick to clubs and—well, mostly clubs. Although I did visit your friend's Occultist's Apothecary shop the other day."

"What?" Diana swallowed the sudden lump in her throat. "You went to see Amara? Please don't hurt her. She—"

Lucien cupped her chin, the hold firm but gentle. "She's fine. I was merely curious as to who you are trying to get to help you defy me. The white witch is a smart choice."

"I didn't go to defy you." She tried to pull away, but he curled one arm around her waist. To anyone walking by it probably looked like they were embracing like lovers, not that she was being held captive by the devil.

"You weren't?" Lucien's sensual mouth was a hard line, and it frightened her a little. Okay, a lot.

"No. I was just freaked out, okay? I'd only just realized the bargain we made wasn't a dream, and it scared me. I needed to talk to somebody who believed in that stuff. I didn't know she was a white witch."

Lucien brushed the pad of his thumb over her bottom lip.

"Lucky for you, I can taste truth." He leaned down and sealed his lips over hers. The kiss was explosive and sinful, open-mouthed with tongue.

Good God... She melted into him, grasping his shoulders to stay on her feet.

When their lips finally parted, she stumbled a little and bumped into the shopping cart.

"Truth." Lucien's lips curved up in a smile. "Good girl. You should never lie to the devil."

"I wasn't trying to lie." She stared into his dark fathomless eyes, wishing she could read his expression. Everything about him was so closed off all the time. He was a dark mystery wrapped in obsidian and buried in fathoms of crushing oblivion. It was easy to become lost in his gaze. It sucked her in, drew her into a black hole where no light could shine. There was just nothingness. A tremor rippled through Diana's body and soul.

Lucien's hands absorbed her shaking, and he suddenly released her, stepping back as he resumed helping her check out. The darkness, the frightening "end" she had sensed just beneath the surface of his gaze had vanished, and once more he looked like an all too sexy man casually shopping for groceries. They checked out, and then they took the cart outside and loaded her trunk. She watched him return the cart to one of the cart kiosks in the parking lot.

"Now what?" Lucien asked.

"We're done. I guess I'll see you next Friday night at midnight." She turned to the driver's-side door and pulled on the handle, but the door didn't open. Because a large masculine hand was pressed on the top of the door, keeping it closed. Tension coiled inside her as she spoke.

"Lucien, I *really* need to go. My parents are expecting me."

"At this *barbecue*?" he asked. There was a hint of a challenge in his tone.

"Yeah." She kept her own voice casual, hoping he wouldn't be interested in coming.

"Then I'll come too."

Shit. So much for the casual plan.

She laughed a little too hysterically. "You can't come to a barbecue. My parents and their neighbors will be there." She gave another fruitless tug on the handle.

"So?" he growled in obvious frustration.

"You can't just—"

"Can't I? Do you forget who you're talking to? I'm the damned devil. I've ended worlds, destroyed empires, and you think you can keep me away from some barbecue?"

Well shit. He has a point. She couldn't stop him from doing anything he wanted to do. That was the problem.

"Okay, you can come, but you have to act normal."

"Right." He chuckled darkly. "Hide the horns and absolutely no stabbing of the guests with my pitchfork." He raked his gaze down her body. "But I might stab you with another kind of pitchfork if you ask me nicely...on your knees."

This time she challenged him with her darkest look. "That is something I have to do *only* on Fridays."

She expected him to be outraged and demand sensual obedience. Instead, he flashed her a wicked, cocky grin.

"You may tell yourself whatever you like, darling, but you like it and me. Soon you will be begging for me on nights other than Friday." He lifted his hand from the top of her car door, and she opened it with relief. That relief was short-lived, however, because he climbed into the car beside her and buckled himself in.

"Please don't do anything crazy to embarrass me or my parents, or scare anyone, for that matter."

He mimed a small cross over his heart. "Promise."

God, this is probably going to be a huge mistake, Diana thought as she turned on the car and pulled out of the parking lot. She couldn't help but think of one of her favorite old movies, *Guess Who's Coming to Dinner.* In the movie, the young woman brings home a man her parents don't approve of because he's black. It was a stunning movie that defied racial prejudices, and it was a powerful love story. But taking Lucien to a barbecue? This was no love story, and he was the devil.

Guess who I'm bringing to dinner?

FOR WHILE I SIT WITH THEE I SEEM IN
HEAVEN, AND SWEETER THY DISCOURSE IS TO
MY EAR THAN FRUITS OF PALM-TREE,
PLEASANTEST TO THIRST. - JOHN MILTON,
PARADISE LOST

L ucien watched the parade of middle-aged couples
entering the front door of Diana's parents' home,
each carrying a tray of food or drinks. They all wore
comfortable-looking clothes. He glanced down at his favorite
suit. Time for a wardrobe change. Closing his eyes, he
snapped his fingers, and when he opened them he had on
jeans and a black T-shirt with the a band logo on it.

"What the—you can't just snap your fingers like that in
public and change clothes!" Diana hissed from the driver's
side of her car. She was staring at him as though he'd grown a
second head.

"I can, and I did," he reminded her smugly. She really
needed to get used to his powers. He hadn't even shown her
the *cool* shit he could do.

"Just don't do anything during the party. Mom and Dad
can't explain your tricks, and it could cause a lot of trouble."

"Fine, fine," he grumbled, and then he got out of the car
and focused on the house. "So this is the residence of Janet
and Hal. The parents."

"Yes." Diana retrieved the groceries from her trunk,

trying to juggle the bags. He deftly removed three of the heavy ones, leaving her carrying one sack of buns.

"Thanks." She stared at the little sidewalk lined with an array of colorful flowers and froze. "What are we going to tell them?"

"Tell them?" He was baffled by the question.

"Yes. I can't just say, 'Hey, Dad, here's Lucien. I made a deal with him to save your life, and now I'm having sex with him. Oh, and did I mention he's the devil?'"

He bit his bottom lip to hold back a bark of laughter. "That would probably give Hal a heart attack. Tell him I'm a boyfriend. One you met in class."

"I'll tell him you're a *friend*," she amended. He could see by the slightly distant look in her eyes that she was already concocting an elaborate story if she needed it.

"Come on." He nudged her in the back to get her moving again. The smells he was picking up from the backyard were quite divine, and he wanted to taste whatever was being cooked.

As they reached the house, a raven-haired beauty in her midfifties met them at the door. Janet, had to be—she looked like a mature version of Diana. He hadn't focused on her at all when he'd first seen her at the hospital. She had been just another mortal to him, but now he was curious. Okay, more than a little curious to meet the woman who'd brought Diana into the world.

"Diana!" Janet embraced her and looked at Lucien expectantly. He cleared his throat.

"This is Lucien Star, Mom. Lucien, this is my mom, Janet."

"It's so nice to meet you, Lucien." Janet held out a hand, and he shook it.

"How do you know Diana?" she asked as he she waved for them to come inside.

"We met in class. He's a friend." Diana shot him a pointed look when her mother turned her back on them as she led them to the kitchen.

Lucien licked his lips at her and winked. The crimson blush staining her cheeks was delicious. He had every intention of getting her alone soon because he wanted to show her exactly what pineapples were for.

After they entered the kitchen, he set the bags of groceries down and then watched Diana and her mother prepare everything. They worked well together, moving in tandem to prepare a fruit salad, a plate of meat patties on a tray, and some veggie dip bowls. It was clear Diana and her mother had done this together many times before. They were talking and laughing, sharing open joy as they worked. Something about that familial intimacy made him go very still inside. The rush of voices and images of the goings-on in hell, the mental reports he received every minute, it all faded to the back of his mind like an old radio turned on in a distant room. For the first time in his existence he was lost, lost in Diana and her world, and he liked it far too much. Andras wouldn't be pleased, but he could stuff it.

I'm the damned devil. If I want to enjoy some vacation time, I can.

"Why don't you and Lucien go outside and set up the tables with the appetizers," Janet said, smiling.

"Okay." Diana hugged her mom and hastily grabbed a veggie tray and shoved it at him. "Take this."

Lucien gripped the tray and followed her out into the backyard. Several men, including Hal, were grouped around the grill cooking hot dogs. Nearby two picnic tables had been set up with red-and-white checkered tablecloths. Several women were drinking tea out of glass Mason jars and laughing as they gossiped. Lucien smirked.

"What are you smiling about?" Diana asked as she leaned

in close to him. The soft natural scent of her skin made his body burn with hunger.

"The secrets," he said.

"Secrets?" Her brows drew together, and he knew he would have to explain.

"I can hear people's secrets. It's part of the gig as the king of hell. When people try to hide things, the easier it is for me to see it. It's almost like I can hear them screaming their secrets loud and clear."

"What kind of secrets?" she asked, her focus on the guests again.

"You really want to know?" He chuckled. She was human, after all, and curiosity was one of those quirky human habits.

"Well, take that man standing next to your father. The one in the loud red Hawaiian shirt." He nodded his head toward a slightly overweight man.

"Jerry Gunter." She nodded. "What about him?"

Lucien's lips twitched. "He likes to put on his wife's shoes and dresses when she's at her girls' martini nights. Calls himself Mrs. Butterfield."

"What?" Diana giggled, and her eyes flashed with laughter.

"But he's a good guy, generally speaking," Lucien added. "Not anyone I'd pay a call to."

"What else?" Diana leaned against him, the little blouse she wore billowing in the breeze, and he was able to catch a glimpse of her gorgeous breasts held in a sensible nude-colored bra. Normally he liked women who wore lacy scraps of lingerie, but there was something about the way Diana wore what pleased her, and not men, that fascinated him.

"Lucien?" She nudged him with an elbow.

"Hmm?" He was still half lost in fantasies of tugging those bra cups down and flicking his tongue against her nipples.

"What else can you see?" She waved a pair of salad tongs toward the people in the backyard.

"All right." He scanned the guests again and then discreetly nodded at a woman in her midforties in a polka-dot black-and-white sundress.

"Mrs. Rafferty," Diana confirmed. "What about her?"

"She's cheating on hubby dearest with his best friend."

"Oh my God," Diana muttered.

"I wouldn't worry. Her husband has a nice little stripper with a heart of gold that he keeps living well in Vegas. He's planning to leave her for the stripper in a few months."

"No way." Diana covered her mouth with one hand, shocked.

"Oh yes, it's going to be quite the fireworks when Mrs. Rafferty finds out about Bethany in Vegas. The cheaters always hate being cheated on."

"But he's cheating too—Mr. Rafferty, I mean."

"He is, but only because wife dearest made him move to the guestroom. He's a lonely man, and Bethany is really a sweet girl."

"Wow." Diana stared at her parents' neighbors with open astonishment.

Lucien sized up the rest of the guests. "Insider trading, has too many cats, secretly in love with the nanny, stealing office supplies..." He ticked off each remaining guest.

"And me?" Diana asked more quietly, her eyes serious.

"You..." He closed his eyes, letting himself embrace the endless flutter of whispers. Secrets flowed like a dark current beneath a river's glassy surface.

"Take me, dominate me, let me taste the dark..."

He opened his eyes, and a slow smile stretched his lips. He leaned in close to whisper in her ear. "Your deep dark secret is *me*." He kissed the shell of her ear. "You want me in every bad way you always dreamed about."

Her little gasps were sweet breathless music to his ears.

"Diana, honey, who's this?" Hal Kingston's voice interrupted what would've been building up to a delicious moment. Lucien had to wipe the glare off his face as he turned to look at Diana's father. He did not like to be interrupted mid-seduction.

"Dad, this is Lucien. He's a friend from one of my summer classes," Diana explained.

"Pleasure to meet you, Mr. Kingston." Lucien held out a hand. Hal removed his grilling mitten and clasped his palm in Lucien's. For a second, recognition flared in Hal's eyes. But a moment later it was gone, buried too deep.

"Have we met? You seem familiar." Hal's puzzled gaze searched Lucien's face for answers.

"I've got one of those faces," Lucien said with a chuckle. Diana shot him a worried and confused glance.

"So you've got classes with Diana?"

"Yes." Lucien grinned because Diana stood slightly behind her father and was dragging her fingers over her throat to signal him to be quiet.

"And what do you do, Mr. Kingston?"

"I run an architecture firm. Or I did, until colon cancer got me. But I'm in remission now and looking forward to going back at work."

"Remission? That's wonderful news," Lucien replied, still ignoring Diana's more frantic attempts to silence him.

"Yeah, I got a second lease on life. So incredibly lucky, you know? I don't ever want to take anything for granted ever again."

Lucien usually didn't like mortals. But there was honesty in Hal's eyes and voice and an innocence that drew him in the same way it had with Diana.

"I'm glad to hear that, Mr. Kingston," Lucien said, and surprisingly he meant it.

"Why don't you kids go and sit by the pool. Hot dogs and burgers will be ready soon." Hal walked back to the grill.

"Kids? He dared to call *me*, the king of hell, a kid?" Lucien growled softly.

"Yes." Diana chuckled. "To him you look like a kid, or at least someone in your late twenties."

"It would explode his little mortal brain to know just how old I am."

"Explode his—no. No exploding, okay? My dad is off-limits, remember?" She shot him a delightfully stern expression that made him want to laugh and then drag her into his arms and kiss her.

And that scared him in a way nothing had except...the fall.

Diana was too dangerous, even to the king of hell.

꧁꧂

DIANA STOOD IN THE KITCHEN CUTTING THE PINEAPPLE Lucien had insisted on serving to the party guests. When she finished, she placed the pineapple rings on a plate and carried them over to the picnic table with the rest of the food. She jumped when someone spoke behind her.

"Diana, you simply have to tell me where you met Mr. Star. He's charming." Diana turned to face Mrs. Rafferty. She eyed Lucien the way a butcher would a fine cow—like she planned to devour him.

"Um...school," she replied slowly.

"School? How young is he? Your age? You're so young." Mrs. Rafferty emphasized the word *young* with open distaste.

"Hmm, he's older than me." Not quite a lie. He was older than her.

"I see." Mrs. Rafferty licked her lips. "I really have to get to know him better."

A sudden flash of jealousy almost knocked the breath out of Diana.

"He seeing someone," she added.

Mrs. Rafferty's eyes narrowed, betraying the saccharine-sweet smile on her lips.

"Oh, honey, I don't care about that."

Sure you don't, Diana thought. *You don't care because you'd climb him like a tree whether he was single or not.*

Mrs. Rafferty headed straight for Lucien, and Diana was tempted to intervene, but she forced herself to stay where she was. Mrs. Rafferty leaned into Lucien, placing a hand on his lower belly in an intimate way. Lucien was smiling, but the longer she talked, the more that smile slipped into a frown, then a heavy scowl. He gripped the woman's wrist and wrenched her hand away from his body, and then he leaned in and whispered something into Mrs. Rafferty's ear. Whatever he said made the woman's face turned ashen.

Then Lucien released her wrist and stalked away from Mrs. Rafferty and toward Diana. He gripped her by the hand and dragged her into her parents' house, searching room by room until he found the bathroom. He closed the door, hitting the lock and sealing them both inside.

"Distract me," he growled, his hands rough and hard as he gripped her waist.

"Distract you? Why?" His eyes were glowing a little red, and his body was hot.

"If I don't get control, the anger will take over and I'll punish that vile woman." His voice was low and raspy.

"You mean Mrs. Rafferty?"

"Yes. *That* vile woman," he spat.

"Okay, let's calm down." She put her hands on his chest, stroking him until he relaxed a little. "What about our next... Friday? Can you tell me what you have planned?"

The frown on his lips twisted up a little. "That is a surprise, you cheeky little thing. I'm not telling."

"See, so much better, right?" she asked.

"I ate the pineapple," he said suddenly, a wicked grin making his eyes gleam.

"What does that have to do with—"

"On your knees and I'll show you." His soft growl was a command, and rather than be angry, Diana was curious. He never forced her to do anything she didn't want to, so maybe she could try whatever he was most definitely looking forward to.

She slowly lowered to her knees, and he cupped her chin, tilting her head back as he peered down at her.

"Open those pretty lips for me." This came out a silken murmur, and Diana couldn't deny that she wanted to do this. *This*...taking him in her mouth. She knew that was what he'd been wanting all along. She just didn't understand how pineapples fit in.

She reached out for his pants, but he waved her hands away. "Hands behind your back."

Doing as he commanded, she waited, knowing what was going to happen...and she wanted it. She'd never gone down on any of her boyfriends. It had never really appealed to her before, but with Lucien? It felt like the hottest thing ever. Her skin was burning up with desire, and her mouth was dry in heady anticipation.

Then he opened his fly and freed his cock. It jutted out, and he gripped it with one hand and her chin with his other hand. Then her own body responded with hunger, her body flushing with a wet heat as a deep, aching pulse started up between her thighs.

She leaned forward, licking the tip of his shaft, and he groaned in soft, husky delight. Then she opened her mouth, and he pushed his cock inside.

"That's it, let me hear those sounds." He began to rock his hips while she sucked on his thick shaft. He forced her to deep throat him, and he twisted one hand in her hair, growling as he pumped harder and harder. She tried to use her tongue to stroke the underside of the shaft, but he chuckled.

"We can work on techniques for sucking me off later. Right now I want to fuck the hell out of your mouth." He was harder, faster, more furious, with anger in his eyes, yet his hand in her hair was gentle. Her nipples pebbled and her womb clenched as shame and desire mingled inside her. She loved him using her, controlling her like this, and she hated that she liked it.

"When you feel me come, swallow when I hit the back of your throat."

Diana made a noise to try to tell him she understood. Then she felt it, the hot spray of his seed as he rammed his shaft totally in, and she choked, desperately swallowing, but she couldn't because of his cock. It shouldn't have been hot, it shouldn't have turned her on to have him use her mouth like a toy, but it did. She was wet and hot for him, and all he'd have to do was touch her clit and she'd explode.

She focused on his taste. He was a little sweeter than she'd expected.

"Fuck." Lucien panted as he slowly withdrew his dick from her mouth. Diana sucked in a breath of air and swallowed his juices.

"You okay?" He grabbed a towel, wiped himself off, and zipped his pants up. Then he knelt in front of her and cupped her face, studying her worriedly.

"Yeah, that was..." She simply had no words. He had just *used* her, and she'd *liked* it.

"Not too rough?" The open concern in his gaze startled her.

"It was rough, but I liked it. I never really wanted to do that with a guy before, but with you it was...*hot*." She thought back over at all. She could've easily pulled away at any point. He hadn't actually had her in a position where she could not have pulled free.

"Do you feel better?" she asked. "Was that distracting enough?" She couldn't believe it, but she was teasing him.

"Oh yes, more than enough. I was outraged by that woman. She thought she could make demands of me. Me! She's lucky I was in a good mood." His scowl was back, but his hands were gentle as he held her face.

Diana hated to admit it, but she was glad Mrs. Rafferty and her come-on attempt hadn't been well received. He'd come straight to her instead, and she'd been relieved and aroused.

"Will you finally tell me about the pineapples?" She reached up to put a hand on his chest.

Lucien chuckled, the rich sound light and almost sweet. It was a sound she'd never heard from him before. She'd grown accustomed to the dark edge of his laughter and wasn't used to this lighter side. She liked both versions.

"A naughty mistress of mine back in the 1970s taught me that consuming fruits or fruit juices, especially pineapple, will make a man or woman's juices sweet."

Diana's face flooded with heat. "You always planned on me going down on you, then?" She wasn't mad. Rather, it was really hilarious, not that she could say why.

"Did it work?" he asked, his voice lowering as he gazed intensely at her mouth.

"Maybe you should taste it." She licked her lips, and he leaned in and lifted her so she straddled his lap on the floor the bathroom. He gave her lower lip a hungry nibble, and she sighed in sheer delight and melted into him. The kiss was lazy and leisurely, and Diana gave over to him and the moment so completely that she forgot where she was. It was like he had all the time in the world and he wanted to spend eternity exploring her mouth. That kind of focus and gentle, sensual intensity made her dizzy and her heart flutter with treacherous emotions too close to affection.

His hands tangled in her hair, gently tugging on the strands as though he needed to get closer to her. He lowered his hands to her back, then down to her ass, cupping each cheek as she arched her body, rubbing against him. He gave her ass a hard squeeze, which made her nipples tighten into points again and her clit throb. This hunger for him felt different than on Friday night. This was real intimacy, a meeting of the souls that left her breathless. But she wondered...did the devil have a soul? Did an angel? There was so much she didn't understand about him or their situation.

A jerk of the doorknob and a curse outside made her and Lucien hastily break apart. She wiped at her mouth, grinning sheepishly as she climbed off his lap and they both got to their feet.

"Just a minute," Diana called, and she knew that whoever was on the other side of that door would know what she and Lucien had been up to. There was only one reason to be in the bathroom at the same time.

They came face-to-face with Mr. Gunter as they exited the bathroom.

"Oh." The man glanced between them, eyes widening.

"Hey, Mr. Gunter," Diana greeted him before she rushed past him. Lucien smiled broadly at the man and slapped his shoulder.

"Nice day for a barbecue, eh?"

"Um...yeah." Mr. Gunter slipped into the bathroom, and Lucien really chuckled as he joined Diana at the back door. Since they'd left the backyard, most of the guests had left and the party was winding down. That was a huge relief because fewer people might guess what they'd been doing. Of course, with the way Diana's face was flaming, it might be obvious anyway.

"Don't regret what we did," Lucien whispered and pressed a kiss to her cheek.

She reached up and touched her cheek, which felt even warmer now from his lips. When she met his gaze, she was again stunned by the softness in his eyes. He was almost like a normal guy, and she felt almost like a normal girl, albeit one who'd gotten away with giving a blow job to the devil at a barbeque.

"You okay with staying just a little bit longer if my parents need me?" she asked Lucien.

"Sure." He glanced around at the remnants of the food and drinks. "I'll grab a drink and wait for you." He headed straight toward the cooler of beers.

Diana found her parents and asked if they wanted her to stick around. When they said no, she turned to find Lucien, but he was gone. Her heart sank, and she couldn't help but wonder if it was because he'd gotten what he wanted and he had no reason to stick around.

She lingered a little longer around the house, tidying up the kitchen before she returned to her apartment. Life had to go on. She could not let Lucien and his schedule dictate her life. This agreement between them lasted only three months. She needed to stay focused on school and not let him disrupt her plans.

To hell with the devil.

✤ 13 ✤

GREAT ACTS REQUIRE GREAT MEANS OF
ENTERPRISE. —JOHN MILTON, PARADISE
REGAINED

"You have a problem," Andras said when Lucien materialized in the location where he had been summoned. They stood in front of an old temple deep in the Amazon rain forest. Roots of ancient trees had broken apart the stone structure built by early humans from a civilization long faded into the obscurity of history. The leafy canopy let sunlight filter down in spirals of light.

"Another one?" Lucien asked. He hadn't wanted to leave Diana or the barbecue. They had so much left to do after their time in the bathroom. He had plans, wicked ones that had been rudely interrupted by Jerry Gunter. He was tempted to assign a succubus to that man.

"We have a croucher," Andras declared with some concern as he pointed to the open doorway made of stone. Old deities, ones almost as old as Father, were carved into the stone, but their identities were unclear because years of rain and moss growth had smoothed out the sharper points of the carvings.

"A croucher? Haven't dealt with one of those since the days of Babylon." Lucien walked closer but froze when the fine hairs on the back of his neck rose in ancient instinctive warning. If he still had his angel wings, they would've been quivering with the need to fly him far away from this place.

"How did you find it? Crouchers don't usually linger in places anymore, and this one is far from civilization." Lucien didn't like this type of demon. It was dangerous, unpredictable, and needed a fair amount of heavenly—or hellish—power to be destroyed.

Andras's blue eyes were cold. "You'll see. This way." He led Lucien around the door, careful not to pass through. The body of a man lay across the stones of a room that no longer had walls. His sightless eyes were wide and still full of terror. His body was cold, but only just, which meant he hadn't been dead long.

"Who is he?"

"An archaeologist. His team rushed back to the base camp to call in the death and have the medical team returning. We need to neutralize the croucher. We can't have it taking any more victims."

Lucien nodded. It was another aspect of his job that people didn't know about. As the king of hell, he had the thankless task of controlling demons, ones in the wild and those in the minds of men. He didn't, contrary to popular opinion, unleash demons on the world. No, they escaped on their own, and he had to drag them back to hell. Croucher demons could be quite nasty. They lingered in the shadows of doorways, and any poor human who passed through would be killed. The Babylonians were the first to discover croucher demons and had named them *rabisu*, or "ones that lie in wait." Crouchers chose doors as their demonic nests because of the powers that entryways held. In every culture in the world, doorways held significance and therefore required protection from malevolent spirits and demons.

Even humans, with their weak instincts, could feel the presence of crouchers.

"I hate these things," Lucien said as he approached the door. The hairs on his neck rose sharply with unsettling tingles, like someone had dripped cold water down his head and onto his neck and back.

"Be careful." Andras stood on the opposite side of the doorway, close to the body of the fallen human. He watched Lucien through the stone frame of the entryway, expecting danger, as he should.

"Brace yourself, Andras. Shit's about to get ugly." Even their father hadn't liked crouchers. He'd warned Cain all those millennia ago that *"sin crouches at the door."*

Andras stood in a ready stance, palms up to summon the fires of hell should they be required.

Lucien slowly reached out to the doorframe. The moment his hand would've passed through the doorway, a shadow slid from the top-left corner of the frame, coiling and twining like an ever-moving spiderweb made of man's most ancient nightmares. Whispers of a thousand tongues could be heard, like a dark Tower of Babel, but Lucien heard every word in each foreign tongue.

Kill, destroy, and consume, death to the light...

Even Lucien didn't want the death of the light. There was no darkness if there was no light.

"Stand and face me, *rabisu*." Lucien reached his hand to the coiling shadows. Pain exploded through his body, knocking the breath from his lungs. He released the fire that burned just beneath his skin and let it float out of his hand and into the shadows.

"Fire..." the croucher's voices whispered in anger.

"Ahh!" Lucien bellowed as the shadows in the doorway expanded around him and he realized his mistake. This wasn't one croucher, but hundreds, maybe a thousand.

"Andras, get out of here!" Lucien screamed. He could just make out the other fallen angel through the fluttering gaps in the shadows.

"No! You stay, I stay." Andras grasped the shadows in his hands and unleashed his own fire. The pain pouring through Lucien was like nothing he'd ever felt in his life...except the day he'd fallen.

He blacked out for a brief second, and all he could hear was the rush of wind as he plummeted into darkness.

When he came to, he was lying on his back, every inch of him bruised and battered, and his ears were ringing. The forest was no longer eerily quiet. The mass of *rabisu* were gone, but not dealt with. They would be seeking other doorways, other victims. He'd failed. He shouldn't have failed. But he had.

"Andras?" he croaked.

He heard coughing as he struggled to sit up, and he caught sight of his friend lying broken and hurt on the opposite side of the door. Andras was worse off than him. He called Andras, but he had no strength to move just yet.

"This way," someone shouted in the distance.

Fuck, the humans were returning to collect their dead man, and they couldn't see him and Andras like this.

Lucien clung to the powers inside him, but it was like holding on to the ends of a frayed rope.

"Hang on," Lucien murmured as he crawled through the doorway to Andras. Then he wrapped his arms around the other man's chest from behind and closed his eyes, using the last of his power to take them somewhere safe.

He glimpsed the inside of Diana's apartment as he and Andras materialized into her living room, and then he blacked out a second time.

DIANA STOOD IN THE KITCHEN, WASHING A FEW PLATES before putting them into the dishwasher, when she heard a loud *crack*! She screamed as two bodies smacked into her living room floor, crushing her coffee table into splinters. Seth, who'd been perched on the counter in front of her, screeched, his fur standing on end as he leapt rigidly from the counter and shot like an orange and white striped lightning bolt for her bedroom. Diana dropped the plate she'd been washing, and it shattered in the sink. She rounded the counter and rushed to the two men—*yes*, they were two men. And one was Lucien. He lay on his back, clutching the body of another man. Both were bruised and bleeding, as though they had been in some sort of fight or explosion. Panic nearly froze her for several seconds before she tried to convince herself it would be fine. Lucien was the devil—he wasn't a normal man who could be hurt.

Diana knelt by Lucien and touched his shoulder gently. "Lucien."

His eyelashes fluttered open weakly, and relief flooded through her at the sight.

"Safe," he murmured drowsily. His eyes, usually darker, were now a honey-brown. They looked...*human*, more than they ever had before. Was that possible?

"Yes, you're safe." She hoped she wasn't lying. There wasn't much she could do if something showed up looking for Lucien and whoever was with him.

"Diana." Lucien tried to lift one hand to touch her face, but it fell back to the ground and his eyes closed.

For several minutes she wasn't sure what to do. She dragged the second man onto the floor beside Lucien and placed pillows under their heads. How was she supposed to take care of a fallen angel?

She pulled out her cell phone and dialed Amara.

"Hello?" Amara's calm voice was a welcome relief.

"It's Diana. I have a situation."

"What's wrong?" Amara's voice rose a little in concern.

"Well...I have two angels...well...Lucien and another, and they just sort of appeared in my apartment. Someone or something beat them up. What should I do?"

"Do they have any open wounds?" Amara asked.

"No, they're just unconscious." Diana peered down at them.

"Then I'm not sure what else you can do. They're immortal. They should heal in time."

"Okay. Thanks."

"Diana, be careful." Amara's gentle warning seemed to mean more than just whatever had befallen Lucien and his fellow angel.

"I will." She hung up.

She finally settled in to do her homework and was halfway through her reading when Lucien moaned and shifted. She watched him, not sure what she could do to help.

"Diana?" he called.

"Yes?" She set her schoolwork down and rushed over to help him sit up against the back of the couch. He wiped an arm across his face, and it smeared the blood on the cut from his cheek. She'd get a towel and clean that up as soon as she had a minute to talk to him.

"What happened?" she asked, examining his eyes. The blackness had crept in a little, but they were still mostly brown.

"Tangled with a croucher demon," he said and sighed heavily. "More than one, actually. Got my ass handed to me."

"A what?"

Lucien tilted his head back, sighing again. The sound was world-weary.

"A croucher demon, a demon that lurks in doorways. The last time I fought one, it was back in Babylon."

"Okay—" Diana had no idea how to respond that. "Are you and whoever that is safe?"

"That's Andras, a prince of hell, one of my friends since before the fall." Lucien's honesty stunned her. He wasn't usually so open about the fall or other angels.

"Are you guys okay? I honestly don't know what to do." She got up and went to the kitchen to wet a towel and returned to him and wiped his face gently. He let her, his brown eyes now halfway between that light brown and the dark almost black she was used to.

"We need to rest. The croucher demon sucks the life force away, and had Andras and I been mortal, we would've died instantly."

Diana gently cupped his chin to make him face her so she could check him for more wounds.

"Do you have to fight these demons often?"

"No, that's what was so dangerous. Normally a croucher is solitary, and yet there were hundreds in this old Aztec temple. They killed an archaeologist who was exploring the ruins."

"What?" Diana paused, wiping some blood from his chin.

"Andras monitors human deaths. It's his job. Suspicious deaths, even when those souls aren't destined for hell, are reviewed by him. He found the dead human, realized he'd been killed by a croucher and brought me in. I've battled them before, but always one at a time. Even between the two of us we couldn't stop so many at once. The group of demons fled the temple, and Andras and I—ended up here." He tilted his head and looked around. "Why are we here?"

"Good question." Diana sat back and stared at him. The king of hell and the prince of hell lay on her floor, completely exhausted from a battle with a bunch of ancient Babylonian croucher demons. Just another typical Saturday night.

"I should help Andras home." Lucien tried to stand, but

he collapsed back to the ground. Diana put a staying hand on his shoulder.

"Why don't you rest. Close your eyes and sleep, or do whatever you need to do to recover. I don't think you're in any shape to go anywhere. Why don't you lie down on the couch?"

She helped him get back up, and he collapsed on the couch. His head fell back, and he closed his eyes. After a minute of watching him, she grabbed a soft fleece blanket from her closet and laid it over him, and then she got a second one for Andras.

"I can't believe I'm babysitting fallen angels on a Saturday night."

Diana returned to her homework. It was only a few hours later when she finished and decided to order pizza even though it was almost ten o'clock. After the day she'd had, she needed it. She picked up her cell phone and was ready to dial when she looked toward the living room. Andras was gone. Only a blanket and his pillow remained. Lucien was sitting up, the blanket pooled around his hips, and he was flicking through the TV channels with the sound muted. How had she not heard him and Andras wake? She must have been zoned out on her schoolwork.

"Lucien? Are you better?" She put the phone down and walked over to him. He looked up at her, his eyes back to the dark, fathomless black again.

"I'm almost my old self. Andras is too. He had duties to resume and couldn't stay to thank you for your hospitality."

"Er...are you sticking around or—"

Lucien chuckled. "So quick to be rid of me, eh?"

"No," she replied instantly. "I was just going to order a pizza if you want to stay. I'll get whatever you like."

"Oh." Lucien seemed generally surprised, and honestly Diana was too. She hadn't thought she wanted to be around him when she didn't have to be, but that was changing. They'd had so much fun at the barbeque, and he'd seemed almost normal.

"So do you..." She held her breath.

"Yes. I like sausage."

"Me too." She retrieved her phone to order the pizza. Then she went to the bedroom to grab another textbook from her shelf. When she came back out, Lucien was standing up and stretching. His clothes were tattered and torn, and he still looked like...well...hell.

"Do you want to use my shower? You can freshen up if you want."

He scraped a hand over his jaw in thought. "I think I will." He headed for the bathroom and started stripping out of his clothes.

Diana didn't move, she just stared at him, watching his glorious naked ass, but she froze when she saw his back and the two scars she'd glimpsed when he'd been swimming in Belize. The sudden need to touch them—to ease the pain that he must have experienced—was overpowering. Before she could think, she closed the distance between them and placed a hand on his back. He stiffened in response, but when she expected him to lash out, he didn't.

"Lucien," she whispered, tracing the knot of scars. "They look so painful."

"They still hurt," he whispered softly and glanced over his shoulder at her, and she saw pain in his eyes.

Diana leaned in and pressed her lips to his shoulder blades, then the scars one by one. Lucien exhaled softly, the sound so *human* that it broke her heart.

I'm falling for him. I'm falling for the devil.

She cleared her throat and stepped away before she did something foolish like getting into the shower with him.

"Shower and I'll order pizza."

He turned on the taps and stepped into the shower, and she headed into the kitchen. She ordered a pizza and lay on the couch, her eyes glued to the TV so she wouldn't think about a naked Lucien in her shower. He stayed in there a good half hour, and she got to the point where she was worrying about her water bill.

When the doorbell rang, she answered it and paid the teenage boy holding a large sausage pizza. Then she opened a bottle of red wine and poured two glasses and prepared two plates. She was carrying them over to the couch when Lucien emerged from the shower dripping wet, a towel wrapped low around his hips.

Oh. My. God. His dark hair was wet, and the ends curled up a bit. He grinned as he caught her staring.

"Uh...pizza's here." She pointed at the coffee table. He started to reach for his towel as though to remove it. She spun away, facing the wall.

"You can look now," he teased.

She slowly looked over her shoulder and saw he was dressed now in jeans and a white T-shirt.

"How—"

He wiggled the tips of his fingers, which reminded her a bit of Samantha from the show *Bewitched*.

"Oh...right." She held out the plate of pizza, and he accepted it. She quickly sat on one end of the couch, and he did the same.

"You want to watch a movie or something?" Diana offered.

"Sure." Lucien bit into a slice and sighed, but the sound was one of relief rather than worry. Diana perused her DVDs and chose a classic movie—*An Affair to Remember*, starring Cary Grant.

When the credits began, Lucien leaned back against the couch and watched with mild curiosity. Diana half expected him to protest her choice and put on a horror movie or a violent action film instead. But he didn't. He ate his pizza, drank the wine she offered, and watched an old romance movie...like a real boyfriend.

I should not go there. I can't think of him like that. He'll never be... We will never be...

She was surprised by how much that realization stung. She hadn't wanted to like him or the way he made her feel, but so much had changed between them since that first night she'd come to him. The cold, unfeeling dark devil was changing into a lighthearted human man. Right now she could almost forget what he really was.

Maybe that was all she would ever have, a night like tonight where she could pretend he was human, that he was hers.

❧

LUCIEN WATCHED THE CREDITS ROLL ON THE TELEVISION screen, and for a long moment he was lost in the story of the lives of the characters. Such loss, such love, such tragedy and redemption. It was a movie of hope and despair in equal parts. The ache in his chest, the one that reminded him he missed heaven, seemed stronger than it had been in many years. He glanced down at Diana, who slept in his arms. At some point they'd stretched out on the couch lengthwise, and she'd fallen asleep.

Lucien had never met anyone so trusting of him. She never ceased to amaze him. A human who trusted the devil. *Really trusted him.* He didn't even really know her, this woman who was changing him from the inside out.

But I want to know her, want to know everything...

He vowed he would ask her a thousand questions when he had the chance.

He closed his eyes and brushed a lock of her hair back from her face as he opened his mind to the past, to the life he'd had in the realm of heaven before he'd fallen. He wanted to give Diana that glimpse and share what the light felt like. She carried so much of his darkness, but this one gift he could give her.

Gleaming spires, music played by divine hands, the glittering of white wings in the sunlight, the endless, vast everything. There was no limit, no end, not there. It was a beginning, a continuation, a journey, a destination. It was home.

Lucien's eyes burned, and when he opened them thick tears escaped. He wiped at them, staring at the wetness on his hands in confusion.

Angels did not cry. The devil definitely did not cry.

Yet here was proof, the salty sheen upon his fingertips. Proof that he was...what?

Getting weaker? Perhaps. After fighting with all those crouchers, it seemed possible. Andras would counsel him to be careful, to make sure that he didn't get attached to a human. Andras would be right. He needed to keep his distance. The king of hell could not afford to grow soft simply because a human woman made him want to feel, to remember. The scars on his back burned with the memory of losing his wings.

I paid my price. Now I'm free, free from caring, free from bowing down, free from obeying.

He looked down at Diana again, studying the way her dark lashes fanned out on her cheeks and the hint of a smile on her lips as though she was dreaming. He bent his head and feathered his lips over hers, and with a faint kiss he whispered to her, "Dream of me, darling. Dream of midnights past and midnights to come. Dream of heaven in my arms." Then he closed his eyes and vanished.

❦

JIMIEL WATCHED THROUGH THE WINDOW AS LUCIEN SPOKE softly to Diana as she slept. Kindness...that was the expression on Lucien's face, but how was that possible? Lucien shouldn't be able to be kind, if that was what Jimiel was seeing. Suddenly there was a flutter of invisible wings beside him, and he spotted Andras next to him on the balcony of Diana's apartment. For a second Jimiel thought he would have to battle his former brother, but Andras raised his hands in the universal sign of peace.

"It troubles me too." Andras nodded at Lucien and Diana.

"What can we do?" Jimiel asked. It was strange to be on the side of his fallen brother after so many years.

"Lucien has a contract. Only Diana can revoke it."

"But when she saw Lucien's lawyer, she learned that if he gets bored with her before the contract ends, Lucien can let her go and her father will be safe."

Andras smirked. "Eavesdropping? Not very angelic, brother."

"I'm her guardian. It's part of the job. I can't *un*hear things."

"I don't think Lucien will tire of her. He's growing more attached, and the attachment is weakening him." Andras scowled. "We fought off a hundred crouchers, and they almost killed us. He's battled much worse in the past with less trouble."

Jimiel watched Lucien suddenly vanish, leaving Diana alone. She reached for him and, finding nothing, made a soft murmur of disappointment but remained asleep.

"What can we do?" Jimiel asked.

"I don't know." Andras's blue eyes seem to burn like ice. "Killing her is out of the question."

"Of course it is!" Jimiel snapped. "Guardian angel, remember? My whole job is to keep her breathing."

Andras chuckled darkly. "And yet you let Lucien make a deal with her. What happened? Take a day off?"

"No. I wasn't watching her at the hospital. She was supposed to be safe there."

Andras shook his head, still grinning darkly. "Well done."

"Shut up," Jimiel growled.

Andras was still laughing when he disappeared. Jimiel sighed and continued his vigil at Diana's window, praying he would think of something. What in heaven was he going to do? But Andras was right—only Diana could break her deal with Lucien, and she wouldn't do that because it would condemn her father to death.

"We're both screwed," the guardian angel muttered to Diana, even though she was too lost in dreams to hear him.

❧ 14 ❧

YET HE WHO REIGNS WITHIN HIMSELF, AND
RULES PASSIONS, DESIRES, AND FEARS, IS
MORE A KING. - JOHN MILTON, PARADISE
REGAINED

T*he third midnight*

DIANA WAS ACTUALLY EXCITED FOR FRIDAY TO COME.

The week had seemed to drag until Friday morning. She'd gotten texts from Lucien, of course, his teasing comments always making her laugh, and she strangely missed seeing him. She woke up early, expecting to see a box on her doorstep, but there wasn't one. Seth sat on the windowsill, his tail swishing as he chattered at the birds outside in the tree near her apartment. His little trilling noises always made her laugh, but today she felt edgy. Why hadn't she gotten her box? She'd always gotten one the morning of their meetings.

Then a thought struck her. Had her plan succeeded before she'd even had time to start? Maybe Lucien was done, had had enough of her and was moving on? It was very possible... and yet she didn't want it to be true. She wasn't supposed to feel that way, but she did. After everything, she liked Lucien, liked being with him, in bed and out. Trusting herself to the devil to save her father was one thing. But falling in love with him? That was a whole other level of stupid.

Diana went through the motions of showering and dressing. She fed Seth and then packed her bag and headed down to her car. She jerked to a stop at the sight of a sports car parked next to hers and the tall dark-haired man leaning against the driver's side, a coffee cup in one hand, a paperback in the other.

"Lucien?" Diana couldn't believe he was here. How long had he been standing there?

"Morning," he replied and sipped his coffee. He finished whatever page he was on and closed the book. She caught sight of the cover.

"*Paradise Lost?* You read Milton?"

"Of course." Lucien chuckled and tossed the book into the space behind his seat. "For a blind man in the 1600s, he had a decent grasp of what happened when I fell. I've always suspected he might've been a prophet."

"A prophet?"

"A human who receives visions from angels. Once an angel falls, we can't see those humans who have the ability to hear heavenly messages. It's Father's way of protecting the prophets. Not that I or any of my fallen brethren have any intention of doing anything to hurt them."

"Right." She honestly had no idea what to say to that. Sometimes when he talked about things like prophets, angels, and demons, she still on some level couldn't wrap her mind around it.

"So... What are you doing here? I don't come to see you until tonight." She was pleased, *really* pleased that he was here, but he'd been absent all week, and she'd feared she might have succeeded in boring him.

"I thought we could take a little trip to London, or maybe Shanghai, grab some food and see how quickly I can strip you of those clothes." He said this all with such a seductive, flirty grin that her knees buckled.

"That sounds great, but I have class until twelve thirty."

"Are you rejecting me for some boring old economics class? Me and an exotic foreign destination?" He cupped her chin and crowded against her a little, making her blood pound with excitement, but she had to remember that class was more important, no matter how much she wanted to run off with him.

"Umm...yes?" She tried not to laugh at the mock wounded expression on his face.

"Dammit. Outfoxed by schoolwork." He frowned, then jerked his head toward his car. "Well get in, I'll drive you to class."

"Seriously?" She stared at the Aston Martin roadster.

"Dead serious. Now get in." He hopped into the driver's seat, and she got in the passenger side after tucking her backpack in the space behind her seat. Then she buckled herself in, and he gunned the engine. Soon they left her apartment complex behind.

By the time they reached campus, she was laughing and trying to hold her hair back from the wind whipping around her head.

"See you after class. I'll be right here." He nodded at the curb facing her building.

"You sure? I mean, I can imagine you have lots of things to do, run hell and all that."

He snickered. "*Run hell and all that*... Yes. I certainly do, but right now you're my priority. Being with you pleases me, and as long as that holds true, you won't be rid of me."

She almost corrected him that after three months the

relationship would be over, but she didn't want to think about that.

"See you in a few hours," she called over her shoulder and headed inside.

"Still with your 'not boyfriend'?" Jim asked when she stepped through the glass doors of the building.

"Yeah." She blushed.

"I still think that the whole situation is iffy." Jim held open the classroom door for her, and she went in ahead of him.

"Our relationship is unique." That was all she was going to say on the matter.

Jim seemed to realize he'd overstepped the boundary and offered her a polite smile. Professor Belkin came into the room, his face pale and his eyes a bit glassy.

"I'm sorry, I'm not feeling very well today. I've posted the lesson online. I will be around this weekend to answer questions. You are dismissed." The professor removed a handkerchief and wiped his brow.

"He doesn't look good," Diana whispered to Jim.

"He definitely doesn't. I heard the flu is going around."

"Is it?" Diana blanched. The last time she had the flu she'd been a wreck for six days.

"Yeah." Jim gathered his books and nodded politely at their professor before he exited the class.

Diana returned all her note materials back to her bag. Just as she was starting to leave, Belkin sneezed as she passed by him. He apologized profusely, but she told him it was nothing to worry about.

When she left the classroom building she expected to have to wait for Lucien, but he was there, the red roadster drawing admiring looks from the guys in her class and Lucien himself drawing hungry looks from her female classmates.

"Done already?" Lucien was surprised as he opened the passenger-side door for her.

"You didn't give my professor the flu, did you?" she asked. Getting a poor man sick so she didn't have class seemed exactly like the sort of thing the devil would do.

He raised one brow in a mute, unamused challenge. "I haven't and would never in future do anything so amateurish. If I wanted to make you skip the class, the reason would be far more dramatic, I assure you."

She studied him, not really believing for a moment that she could trust his expression. He was the devil, after all, but he did seem to make sense. The devil would definitely go for something big and dramatic if he wanted to cancel class.

"So my plans are back on then?" he asked hopefully.

"I guess they are." She smiled a little. "But if you plan for us to stay anywhere overnight, I'll need my—"

"Bag, yes I know. What do you have in that bag? The Holy Grail?"

"Ha ha." She snorted. "I'm a girl. We need things if we stay overnight. Guys have no clue what it takes to not look like crap the next morning."

Lucien chuckled as he started his car. "Women have always been high maintenance. Even Adam's wife, Eve, in the garden of Eden was always fussing about her hair."

She stared at him. "Eve was real?"

"Of course. Well, she wasn't actually named Eve, nor was the first man named Adam, those names came later. It was really before men had a defined language. Much of the Bible is allegory and metaphor, you see. Except for the stories about me. No exaggeration there."

Diana put on her seat belt and tried to digest everything he was telling her.

"If I spend the rest the day with you, I want to ask a bunch of questions, and you need to answer them."

"Oh." He laughed darkly. "Getting all demanding. I like this side of you. Maybe you can demand that I pull the car over and fuck you right here." He licked his lips in a way that made her body quiver with longing. She had to fight very, very hard to not do exactly that.

"We have time for that later," she reminded him.

He threw back his head, sighing dramatically. "Very well, but I have questions too, about you. You answer mine, I'll answer yours. Fair deal?" He offered her one hand.

"Deal." She shook his hand.

"See? Making deals with me is quite easy." He winked at her, and then they hit the road.

"What is something you've always longed to see?" Lucien asked as they got back to her apartment.

"Um...I don't know. It's a huge list, really."

"Then pick one and we'll start there." He grinned mischievously.

"I guess the Monarch Butterfly Biosphere Reserve, but that's in Mexico."

Lucien rolled his eyes and curled an arm around her waist as they walked up to her apartment door.

"Snap of my fingers, remember? I can take you anywhere."

Diana couldn't believe he actually wanted to do this for her, but she wasn't going to look that gift horse in the mouth.

"We will go where you wish today. And at midnight, I get to do *whatever* I want to you."

A delicious shiver of longing rippled through her as her imagination ran wild at the thought of what he might want to do to her.

"Okay. I think that sounds like a good trade," she teased, but her heart was racing. She wanted midnight instantly, yet she also wanted to spend the day seeing amazing things with Lucien.

She unlocked her apartment and went inside to make sure

Seth had plenty of food, and then she returned to her living room. Lucien had closed her apartment door but was still holding on to the doorknob.

"Ready for Mexico?" he asked.

She nodded and walked toward him just as he turned the handle. When he opened the door, she gasped. There was a massive forest spread out all around them, and the trees were...moving. No, not the trees—the butterflies covering every inch of every trunk for miles. The black-and-orange wings of millions of butterflies flapped as they took refuge in the trees in the reserve. Sunlight spilling through the canopy illuminated patches of monarchs here and there in spots of gleaming, rippling gold. Small clusters of monarchs took flight, dancing in circles before resettling on another tree.

Diana swallowed hard as she fought to control her emotions. She had never seen anything so beautiful in her life.

"Why here?" Lucien asked as he came up to stand beside her. "Why butterflies?"

Diana held out a hand as a butterfly flew past, and it landed on the back of it. She looked at the insect and then Lucien, trying to compose her words. It was almost impossible to explain.

"You're immortal. You never die," she said. "But I will... someday. All things in this world die except for you. Death is frightening and permanent. When I see something so fragile, so beautiful, and I see it has only a short life, it makes me appreciate its beauty all the more. Like snowflakes. You catch one and you have but a few seconds to see the intricate, one of a kind pattern before it melts away. There's a tragic perfection in that. I don't know if I'm explaining this well..." She tried to ignore the heat flaming her face.

"I think I understand." Lucien was watching her, not with hunger, not with wicked intent, but with a sort of sorrow and true understanding that made her heart ache. Did he know that he'd once been a beautiful thing, unique and precious to God before he'd fallen? Diana couldn't but wonder if he ever thought of it. Or perhaps he thought too much of it, and the reason he basked in the darkness of his existence was to forget the world of light he'd come from.

"Everything on the earth has the potential for beauty," she continued. "The mountains that will last long after I'm gone and this butterfly whose lifespan is only an instant compared to mine. Life itself is beautiful, eternal. It always goes on, always renews after death. It's a promise that there is no true ending of things." The monarch took flight, and Diana sat down in the thick grass beside one of the trees and watched the butterflies. After a long moment, Lucien eased down beside her. She reached over and covered his hand with hers, and to her relief he didn't pull away.

"When I was..." He cleared his throat. "Before I fell, I used to love the earth and the riches of life here. It's so easy to become blinded by rage and hatred and forget to see beauty."

"Lucien, why did you fall?" She'd heard all the myths—the devil had his pride, the devil was jealous—but she wanted to see and hear his perspective.

He watched the forest and the monarchs for a long time before he responded.

"Fear. I fell because I was afraid. Father created the universe and the angels. I thought he was content with us, but I was wrong. He made humanity, and I saw that his love for humans was stronger than his love for me. I was afraid his love for me would fade and that I would become nothing in the universe. Hate and anger always come from fear. And I feared humans more than anything because they lessened my own relevance to my father." He turned his hand over so that their hands could link, and he laced his fingers through hers, staring at their joined palms.

"Everyone needs to have a purpose and to feel loved. That makes you human." She pointed this out softly, hoping it wouldn't upset him. She brushed the tips of her fingers over his palm with her free hand, trying to show him that she cared.

"Me, human." He shook his head ruefully. "What gives you a purpose? What drives you, Diana?"

For a long moment she didn't answer. She continued to stroke her fingers over his hand, admiring the powerful, elegant fingers entwined with her own.

"I like to design houses. I love architecture. It's about giving someone a place so they can come back at the end of a bad day, or a great day, and feel safe and at ease with their surroundings. I want to be the person who creates not just houses, but *homes*." She took in the dancing butterflies around her as she came to a realization. Home didn't have to be a place, not always. Sometimes home could be a person you loved. She glanced up at Lucien. His eyes were half-closed as though the pleasure her touch was giving him was soothing, like a cat stretched out on the carpet beneath a band of sunlight.

"Now it's my turn," he said. "If you were trapped on a desert island, what movie would you watch?"

His question surprised her, and she laughed. The sound startled several nearby butterflies, and they took flight in a dazzling display of orange and black.

"You're asking me a desert island question?"

"Yes, why is that so funny?" he demanded, his gaze betraying that he was a little hurt at her amusement.

"It's...never mind. Why would I bring a movie to a desert island? I wouldn't have anything to watch it on."

"Very well, a book then?"

She tapped her chin thoughtfully. "*Twilight*."

"No. Absolutely not," he growled.

"What? You don't like vampires?"

"Actually, I don't. They're all broody and dramatic."

"Amara said vampires are real. Is that true?" she asked. It had been one of her burning questions.

"Yes, and so are werewolves and a lot of other...things."

"Wow."

"So, any book other than *Twilight*. What would it be?"

"*The Historian*, by Elizabeth Kostova." She bit her lip to hide a smile as he suddenly frowned, and before she could react, he pounced on her, tackling her back on the soft grass, pinning her beneath his masculine body.

"Another vampire book? Do I need to manifest some fangs and bite your pretty neck to arouse you?" He licked his lips and leaned down to kiss her neck. She squealed when he nipped her throat just hard enough to feel his teeth. And to her shock, a flood of wet heat pooled between her thighs.

"Interesting," Lucien murmured as he nibbled her earlobe.

She moaned as he moved his lips to hers and explored her mouth with a slow, decadent kiss. The kiss was sweet yet sinful, and she couldn't deny that this man, this fallen angel, filled her with a wild lust. She knew that to tempt him was dangerous, not physically but emotionally. The more time she spent around him, the more addicted to him she became.

Their lips parted briefly, and she raised her lashes to gaze into his eyes.

"Can you take me anywhere?"

He nodded.

"Would you take me somewhere you love?"

He stared at her for a long moment, then nodded solemnly. They vanished from the forest of butterflies in an instant. When she opened her eyes again, they were deep within a canyon. The night sky was dark and endless above them. All around them stood people holding luminaria candles. The crowds moved slowly, people walking one by one to stand in front of the entrance to an ancient city, where they placed the candles on the sand. Gold circles of light blossomed like thousands of massive lightning bugs along the sand. The collective glow illuminated the entrance to a building carved into the stone wall of the canyon.

"This is...Petra. In Jordan," she gasped softly.

"It is," Lucien said. "They sometimes hold night concerts. Tonight is one of those nights." He curled an arm around her waist and led her back toward the edge of the crowd. Then they sat down on the sand next to several other people to wait. The canyon rustled with the whispers of the crowd, making the ancient façades of Petra come alive with ghostly whispers. They stood directly in front of the most famous carved part of the ancient city, Al-Khazneh.

Then a man stepped out of the doorway of the carved stone edifice, and a hush fell over the crowd. The candles flickered, and everyone watched as the man waved at them in greeting. He stood solemn and silent for a heartbeat, and then he began to sing. His voice carried the notes of a familiar opera, and it was both haunting and beautiful. The music of the song echoed through Petra and the canyon, spinning spells of arias and firelight from the luminarias.

Diana leaned against Lucien's side, resting her cheek on his shoulder as she listened to the man sing. After a moment Lucien wrapped an arm around her, and in that moment Diana knew without a doubt that she'd fallen in love with him. He'd brought her to a place that he loved, and it was ancient and beautiful, full of quiet reverence. There was no evil here, no schemes, no crossroads bargains or demons. It was only them, the light of the luminarias, and the haunting beauty of an opera being sung. It was a holy moment, one she knew she would carry deep in her heart for as long as she lived. When there were no more midnights to meet him, when she was old and gray and living a quiet life, *this* would always be in her heart. And he would never know, could never know how she'd fallen in love with him.

I fell for the angel, not the devil.

❧ 15 ❧

THE MIND IS ITS OWN PLACE, AND IN ITSELF
CAN MAKE A HEAVEN OF HELL, A HELL OF
HEAVEN. —JOHN MILTON, PARADISE LOST

L ong after the opera singer had left and the candles were extinguished, Lucien held Diana in his arms, soaking in the moment and memories of this place. Petra had always been one of his favorite places. Funny, he hadn't been here in years, but he had heard about the concerts somehow, and that had lingered in the back of his mind. When was the last time he'd done something simply because he wanted to? Something pure, something without repercussions in the universe that would draw the wrath of his winged brothers?

Diana sighed softly, and the sound was dreamy and relaxed.

"That was...amazing." She turned in his arms and leaned up to kiss his cheek. A wild pulse of electricity seemed to shoot through his body at the point where his lips touched hers.

"That's only the beginning of what I would like to show you."

"Oh?" Her eyes brightened, and he nodded.

"This way." He nodded toward the doorway that led

inside Al-Khazneh. The moment they reached the entry, he drew open a ripple in the structure of the earth's plane of existence and connected them to another location. They stepped through in the blink of an eye onto moss-covered ground. Diana's gasp was full of delight as she spun around.

"Where are we?"

All around them wooden beams were crafted to hold up the large ancient branches of a wisteria tree. Purple flowers cascaded down in enchanting waterfalls. Ground lights illuminated the flowers from below, while fading sunlight danced through the blossoms from above.

"Welcome to Ashikaga Flower Park in Tochigi, Japan."

"Japan?" She whispered the word in shock. "How on earth do..." She half smiled. "I need to stop asking that."

"I would try to explain, but it's like a fish explaining how breathing underwater works to a bird."

"Right. I love wisteria." She spun around beneath the tree as a light breeze stirred the branches. "It's so whimsical, you know?"

"Whimsical?" He chuckled. He had never had occasion to use that word before.

"Yeah, whimsical." She opened her arms. "Want to dance?"

"There's no music, and I do not dance, at least not the kind I think you're wanting me to do." He licked his lips, picturing how he'd love to grind his hips against hers in the most erotic way beneath strobe lights while music thumped rhythmically all around them.

"We don't need music. Come on, please?"

Lucien walked toward her, stunned that he was even doing this, but she'd begged so sweetly.

"You're going to owe me so much in bed, darling," he said, grinning.

"Very well, you seductive bastard, do what you want tonight. Right now I want to dance," she teased.

He placed one hand on her lower back, and she wrapped her arms around his neck, holding on to him. Their bodies were pressed flush to each other, and despite the lust racing through his veins that demanded he lay her flat and take her here, he wanted to dance too. She closed her eyes, and they started to slow dance. He'd never understood until tonight why anyone would want to dance this way.

The breeze moved the blossoms and made them whisper, and the wood creaked as the branches swayed. Distant birds sang as twilight fell, and they danced beneath it all. His throat tightened as he realized the scents in the air were heavier than usual, that the sounds were clearer and the heat of Diana's body was warmer. He'd never been so aware of himself physically before. Dancing this close, this slow was too intimate. He felt vulnerable.

A tear escaped his eye, and he shakily rubbed it away, stunned. He shouldn't be feeling like this. Had something in him weakened? Was that why he had been unable to fight off the croucher demons? He'd failed for the first time in his existence to destroy rogue demons—and it had been because this human was making him soft. Too damned soft.

He broke away from Diana and muttered an apology, then cursed himself silently. The devil didn't apologize. The devil wasn't sorry...but he was.

"Lucien?" She whispered his name in concern.

"I'm...sorry," he muttered, and in a blink they were back in her apartment, and in another flash he was gone.

☙❧

LUCIEN HAD VANISHED AGAIN. DIANA COLLAPSED ON HER couch, and Seth curled up beside her, purring loudly.

"What the hell am I doing?" she whispered as she scratched at Seth's ears. He half-closed his eyes with pleasure. This was nuts. She was in love with Lucien. Stupid, bad idea as it was, it was too late. She loved him. Not the devil part of him, but the other part, the man who loved concerts by candlelight in ancient Jordanian cities and dancing beneath wisteria blooms in Japan. She loved the angel with the missing wings and awful scars.

"Seth, I'm so screwed." She set the cat on the floor, grabbed her car keys from the table, and headed outside.

She drove straight to Amara's bookshop and was relieved to see her friend selling a few books to a woman. Diana waited for the woman to finish paying before she rushed over and hugged Amara.

"Oh dear. More tea, then?" Amara chuckled gently.

"I swear I'm not pathetic, but it's just...I need to talk to somebody."

Amara nodded. "I understand. I'll put the kettle on, and we'll talk."

As they sat down, teacups in hand, Diana confessed, "I'm in love with him."

"Him? You mean..." Her dark brows winged up in surprise.

"Yeah. *Him*."

Amara was silent for a long moment. "Does he know your feelings?"

"I don't think so. Each time things seem to get... emotional, he bails."

"He does?" With elegant fingers, Amara played with a string of black beads that hung around her neck, and Diana was strangely comforted by the sound of the beads clicking softly against one another. It was a normal sound in a world that had been turned on its head.

"You have two more months owed to him on your contract?"

Diana nodded. "Yeah."

"Then you must stay the course. If you love him, you love him. Either he will come to see it and appreciate that, or he will not." Amara reached across the table and gripped one of Diana's hands. "You can and will survive a broken heart."

A headache pulsed in Diana's head just behind her eyes, and she winced, touching her temples.

"You okay?" Amara asked.

"Yeah, I just have a headache." Diana sipped her tea, hoping to relax. It had to be stress-related.

"Why don't you go home and rest. You're seeing him tonight at midnight, yes?"

"That's the plan," Diana said, but she honestly was starting to feel ill. Maybe she really did need to rest.

"Go home, child. Call me if you need anything." Amara slipped her a paper with her number on it.

"Thanks."

Diana stepped out into the late-afternoon sunlight. Dark clouds were gathering in the distance, and the fine hairs on the back of her neck rose. Something wasn't right. She could sense it, *something* in the air, but she wasn't sure exactly what was wrong.

She got into her car and headed back to her apartment. She needed to get some sleep. All would be well. Tonight she had to meet Lucien again, and maybe they could talk about her feelings. She laughed. Yeah, there would be no talk of love, not when she spent her midnights with the devil.

❧

"WHERE IS SHE?" LUCIEN GROWLED AT HIS DRIVER.

"I don't know. She didn't come down to the car. I waited

almost an hour. The lights in her apartment were dark, and I even went up and knocked. No one answered."

Lucien stared at the single white feather in a glass box. It floated gently on wings of magic, soft celestial dust glinting like sparkles in the snow-white feather. Gazing upon the feather always filled him with a mixture of joy and pain.

My last remnant of the days before the fall.

"Thank you for checking on her, Douglas" he finally told the driver. "You may go. I'll handle things tonight."

"Yes, Mr. Star." The human hastily exited Lucien's penthouse. Once he was alone, he closed his eyes and called upon his powers. In a flash, he was in Diana's apartment, but it left him feeling a little dizzy. His powers weren't as strong since the croucher attack, and he had no idea how long it would take to recover. It was dark and quiet, the air hot and stifling.

"Diana?" he called. When he received no response, he rushed into her bedroom and froze. Diana lay in bed, shivering violently beneath the mountain of blankets. He approached the bed and placed the palm of his hand against her forehead. His hand came away covered in cold sweat.

She was ill. *Badly* ill. How was that possible? Then he snarled. Her professor had cancelled class this morning due to an illness.

"Jimiel!" he hissed.

"What?" the guardian angel responded as he suddenly appeared on the opposite side of the bed.

"You let her get sick, you winged moron!" Lucien waved his hand at her body. She was asleep, deeply asleep in the way only an illness could leach someone's energy to the point of being nearly unconscious.

Jimiel's eyes were hard. "I didn't let her. I was avoiding you and wasn't there to see her become infected."

Lucien tilted his head, sensing a lie, but he couldn't fathom why a guardian angel was lying to him.

"Make her better, then."

Jimiel shook his head. "The illness must run its course."

Lucien glanced at Diana again. She was pale and still trembling. Seeing her like this, vulnerable and hurting, filled him with rage.

"Fine, I'll do it." He pressed one hand to her cheek and opened himself to his powers. Usually they came out in a rush, but this time they came out only in a trickle. It wouldn't be enough. He *was* getting weaker; Andras was right.

He turned to shout at Jimiel, but the angel was gone.

"Lucien?" Diana had been healed enough that she was awake, and she was gazing at him.

"It's all right, I'm here." He felt the need to reassure her, to let her know she wouldn't suffer this alone. When he'd fallen from heaven, he'd been completely alone. Hurt and suffering, he'd clawed his way out of the crater toward Eden, and he would have given anything to have someone there to comfort him. He would not let Diana face this alone. She was still sick, still weak. And he couldn't bear the thought of leaving her.

"I missed the car," Diana murmured drowsily.

"You did," he replied as he stroked away the strands of her hair. She was covered in sweat.

"Are you mad? You won't..." She drew in a shaky breath. "Hurt my dad?"

"No," he vowed. He would not punish her for her guardian angel being an asshole. If Jimiel wasn't careful, he was going to smite that bastard.

"What can I do?" Lucien asked. He wanted to heal her further, but he was still weak from his battle with the croucher demons.

"I'm cold and sweaty," she said and sighed unhappily.

"What about a hot shower?" he offered.

"Yeah, that might be nice." She struggled to get the blankets off, and he rolled his eyes and helped her out himself. Then he scooped her up in his arms and carried her into her bathroom. He held on to her by the waist after he set her down. Then he turned on the shower. She pulled at her clothes but was too tired, so he helped remove her shirt and panties. She seemed too tired and sick to care that she was naked. He had turned the shower on, and she leaned against the wall, sighing as the hot water hit her.

"Lucien, could you help me? I'm so sorry," she whispered. Her eyes were pleading, and he couldn't say no to her.

He stripped out of his clothes, stepped inside the shower with her, and helped her wash. She leaned into him, her body still shaking, and he took gentle care with her as he washed her hair and body. He wanted to remember her like this, needing his help, needing *him*. No one had ever needed him before. They needed his power, his deals, his devil bargains, but no one had ever needed *the man* before.

"Are you sure you're really the devil?" Diana laughed softly as he helped rinse the conditioner out of her hair.

"I'm quite sure." He grinned at her.

"You're being awfully nice." She pressed her cheek to his shoulder and wound her arms around his back.

"I plan to collect a few favors from you in bed once you're well," he assured her and gave her ass a playful squeeze.

Another soft laugh escaped her, and the sound made his blood sing.

"Stay there and let me get towels," he said. He made sure she wouldn't fall before he let go of her, and then he climbed out of the shower to grab some towels. Then he turned the water off, slung a towel over his hips, and helped her out. He took his time drying her off and brought her underwear and a large T-shirt. While she dressed, he made a soft nest of blankets on the couch, and then he made her lie down in the nest while he stripped her bed of the sweat-soaked sheets, and with a bit of direction from her, he put them in the washing machine.

When he returned to the living room, she was passed out, but she looked *better*. He sighed and glanced at his soaked briefs. He still had enough power for the small things like quickly drying his clothes, but he couldn't heal her.

He knew he could leave now that she was feeling better, yet he didn't want to go. After a long moment, he approached her bookshelves and studied her books. Then he slid one from the shelf and walked back to the couch. He lifted her up as he sat down so her head lay across his lap. Then he opened the book and read. He wanted to know everything about Diana, how her mind worked, and if that meant he had to read her desert island choice of books, then so be it. He would read *Twilight*. But if any of his fallen brothers found out, they would laugh their asses off. So it would have to be their secret.

"The things I do for you, little human." He brushed the back of his knuckles over her cheek, enjoying the velvet-soft feel of her skin, and then he turned his focus back on the book.

Hell help me, I'm reading about teenage vampires.

❧ 16 ❧

LONG IS THE WAY AND HARD, THAT OUT OF
HELL LEADS UP TO LIGHT. - JOHN MILTON,
PARADISE LOST

T here were times when Diana was too cozy to ever want to move. This was one of those moments. She was warm and safe, and a wonderful piney sent clung to her as she shifted in her blanket cocoon.

She tensed when something beneath her grunted.

What? She opened her eyes, blinking against the sunlight. She was lying on Lucien's lap on the couch.

"Sorry," she murmured.

"It's quite fine. I didn't need that particular rib you jabbed," he teased. His eyes were halfway between obsidian black and soft brown. What made his eyes change? She couldn't help but wonder. She saw the book he held in one hand. His other was tangled in her hair, lightly stroking it. The caress felt so good. If she'd been a cat, she would have purred.

"Team Jacob or Team Edward?" She bit her lip, trying to contain the sudden urge to giggle.

"Uh..." He glanced at the book. Good God, the devil was turning bashful?

"Edward, I suppose. I can identify with him. No soul,

corrupting an innocent young woman, feels like he's a damned devil, yada yada. I was *very* bored while you slept."

"Uh-huh." She knew he was lying. He'd nearly finished the book. "I am going to go to the bathroom, and you can finish it. It will be our little secret, I promise." She untangled herself from the blankets and headed into the bathroom. When she chanced a peek over her shoulder, she saw him devouring the book again. Diana let loose a fit of giggles, not caring that he could hear her. Then she ran a brush through her hair and washed her face. She still felt tired, but no longer bone-weary. Her muscles ached from all the chills and the shivering, but she definitely felt stronger.

When she came back out, she found him taking the book back to the shelf.

"There are more?" he asked casually.

"Yeah. You're welcome to borrow them." She started toward him but then realized she was wearing nothing but a T-shirt and panties. Even after the few times they'd had wild sex, she still felt shy around him, especially after he'd just seen her sick as a dog and looking her worst. She spun away to go change, but he spoke.

"Running away?" he asked. His brows held that hint of darkness, one that made her tremble with longing.

"Umm..."

"You don't need to hide from me, Diana." He crooked a finger at her, and she came slowly toward him. He still wore his signature black suit and red tie. She wanted to strip him naked. She may be tired, but she felt good enough to want him. Her pulse quickened with longing.

"Do you still want me, Diana?" He spoke her name again, and it sent delicious shivers through her.

"I do." She came up to him and gripped his red silk tie. "We missed midnight."

"We did," he agreed.

"You make love in the sun?" she asked, half teasing.

"I do." His serious gaze was burning with lust, but there was something softer, sweeter shadowing his eyes that intrigued her.

The devil could have...affection? The danger about him had always drawn her in, but now the softer side was keeping her entranced. She wet her lips with her tongue, and he tracked the movement with his eyes.

"Do you feel well enough?" he asked quietly. "I wouldn't—"

She yanked on his tie, pulling his head down to hers, and stole his lips with a heated kiss. His breath whispered over her lips a moment before they broke apart.

"I want to torture you with pleasure. Will you let me?" he asked.

"Define torture." She kept a hold on his tie and nuzzled his throat, flicking her tongue against his skin. He tensed and suddenly cupped her ass. She squealed as he lifted her up, and she gripped his shoulders and wrapped her legs around his hips as he carried her to the bed. When he dropped her onto her back, she caught the fresh scent of laundry.

"You washed the sheets? Let me guess—you snapped your fingers, and it was done just like that?"

He shook his head as he stripped off his coat and tie. "I guess you don't remember coaching me on how to use the washer. You were pretty out of it. I thought you'd appreciate the grand gesture of me not taking the easy way out." He stared at her just as he was rolling up his sleeves.

"Oh God, that's fucking hot," she said.

"Me or the laundry?" His voice was edged with seductive danger. It only made her hotter.

"Both, oh my God, both." She scooted back on the bed as he turned and dug in her drawers for...pantyhose?

"I'm tying you up," he growled softly, and she only struggled a little as he tied her hands to the headboard. He knelt between her thighs, and with one strong jerk of his hand, he ripped her panties off.

"Mortals." He laughed darkly, the sound rich and sinful. "I will *never* understand you." Then he tossed her destroyed panties off the bed and pushed her thighs apart, baring her to his gaze. Strong hands gripped her inner thighs, keeping them wide open, and she trembled, knowing she couldn't stop him from doing whatever he wanted.

He gazed down at her, his brown eyes black like obsidian again.

"Slow and gentle...or hard and fast?" he growled softly. The sound was almost animalistic, almost demonic. She would've said slow and gentle, but she was *hurting* for him, and she knew she could take it if he went hard. She *wanted* that frenzied lust. She wanted him to wreck her for all other men.

Devastate me. Break me, the dark voice in her mind begged him. By the red flashing of his eyes, she knew he'd heard her thoughts.

He moved back on the bed, kneeling over her spread thighs as he placed soft, slow kisses on her belly, then her mound. When his lips fastened on her clit, she whimpered at the excessive pleasure overtaking her. He was cruel with his tenderness, because she needed him to be rough, to take her hard and fast. Instead he was toying with her.

"Lucien, please..." She writhed beneath him, his mouth exploring her mound with flicks of his wicked tongue.

He gave her ass a sharp slap, and the light pain felt so damn good that her eyes blurred with tears. The bindings bit into her wrists as she struggled.

"You're like a damn fantasy," he rasped as he licked her slit. Her body responded with a flood of heat.

"The things I want to do to you..." He inserted a finger

inside her, stroking her before he pulled out the soaked digit and sucked her juices off, licking his lips as he did so.

God, he knew just how to set her on fire. He continued to stroke her, sending her into shivers of pleasure. Her thighs quivered with exhaustion and desire.

"Lucien…"

His lips curved up.

"Lucien," she said again in a ragged breath.

"Yes, pet?"

Pet. She hated and loved the word. He caressed her channel, spreading his fingers wide and stretching her.

"I need you." She arched her hips.

"Tell me *exactly* what you want," he commanded.

She was going to have to say it. He was going to make her.

"I want you to fuck me."

Lucien's arrogant smile only made her burn hotter.

He pressed his thumb over her clit, caressing it so she exploded with a hard and fast climax.

As she drifted down from the explosion of pleasure, she watched him through hooded eyes as he pulled her shirt up to her collarbone, exposing her breasts. He played with them, pinching her nipples and cupping and kneading the heavy, aching mounds. Then he unfastened his pants and dropped them to his knees. He hadn't worn anything underneath, so his cock jutted out, thick and long. The sight made her whole body quake with new hunger.

"I can do whatever I want to you, and you like that idea, don't you?" Lucien's voice was dark and rough. The sweet, playful man was gone, and he was the devil she'd seen that first night. The devil who'd scared and thrilled her had returned.

"Answer me."

"Yes," she whimpered, trying to lift her hips, hoping to entice him to enter her.

Lucien's grin widened, and he gripped his shaft, pushing the tip inside her. She held very still, trying to be good and patient. It seemed to amuse and please him. He rewarded her with a sharp, hard thrust. He filled her completely, stripping away everything but her need and his. Lucien bent over her, gripping the headboard, and fucked her. The tendons on his neck stood out in sharp relief, and he breathed hard and erratic as he plunged into her over and over.

In that moment Diana was truly wrecked. In the last few weeks, she'd become a prisoner of his desires and hers. There was no going back to normal life, not after this, or him. She locked her legs around his waist, making him as much a captive as she was to their mutual desire. The pupils of his eyes were still red with an inner fire. She stared deep into them, searching for the angel, not the devil.

All the while, he stretched her, his shaft relentlessly thrusting into her, bringing them together in an ancient dance of flesh and sounds of ecstasy. The delicious friction and the heat of their bodies finally overwhelmed her. She climaxed, making a soft moan of half pleasure, half pain. He came seconds later, a feral brutish cry leaving his lips as the madness between them dissolved into a lethargic mutual exhale. He collapsed on top of her, his face resting on the mounds of her breasts as he panted. Sweat fused their bodies together, and Diana didn't want to move ever again.

"Diana," Lucian murmured her name, that unexpected tenderness coiling tightly around her heart.

"Yes?" She barely had the strength to talk, yet she had never felt so wonderful in her entire life.

He lifted his head so their eyes met. "You aren't like any human I've ever known." There was a bewilderment on his face that made her heart flip.

"Is that bad?" she asked.

He shook his head slowly. "You're the only true *good* thing I've ever had since the fall."

His eyes were that soft, warm shade of brown she loved so much, and she couldn't help but wonder if what he'd said was as close as she would get to a declaration of affection.

I will take it and him any way that I can.

He freed her, kissing her bruised wrists before he cuddled her against him on her bed. His pants were still down, her shirt up, and she would've laughed at the ridiculousness of it, but she couldn't find the strength to care.

"Will you stay?" she asked, rubbing her cheek on his chest. His white dress shirt smelled like him, dark, exotic, with a hint of pine.

"I'll stay." There was a softness in those words, as though he meant far more than just tonight, but she was too afraid to hope that was true. She couldn't have a life with him, not the one she'd dreamt of having. But she could have this, and perhaps a few more midnights and mornings like it before it ended.

She closed her eyes, surrendering to sleep, Lucien's body providing all the warmth she needed. Everything was simply perfect. She wouldn't think about the future or the contract. She would only think of this moment. That was all that mattered.

❧ 17 ❧

The seventh midnight

DIANA ADMIRED HERSELF IN THE FULL-LENGTH MIRROR, loving the knee-length midnight-blue dress that Lucien had sent her in her box tonight. It was like something Grace Kelly would have worn, with a full skirt and an understated elegance.

It's something I would wear if I had a choice, and he knows it.

So much had changed since that night they'd made love her in bed. Things were full of light in a way she couldn't explain. Each kiss they shared, each touch, seemed to ignite her soul with a blinding cosmic light that sent her rushing headlong into his arms, searching for that taste of heaven again and again. Even though there were moments of dark-ness in his eyes, the brown hue was stronger now, the black receding. She'd learned since then that the brown was his more angelic side. That was the man she loved, not the black-eyed creature who'd bought her soul all those weeks ago.

Her phone buzzed in her pocket, and she pulled it out.

Asshat: Looking forward to tonight. Be ready for me, sweetheart.

She couldn't help but grin as she paused before responding.

Diana: I'm always ready for you.

With a giggle she added a pineapple emoji. Her phone buzzed a second later.

Asshat: You're killing me. I'm sending the car early. I don't want to wait, and we have a special reservation tonight. Opera tickets to see *Don Giovani* at the Met.

Diana bit her lip, still smiling.

Diana: You know I love that opera.

Asshat: Of course I know. I've made it my mission to know everything about you.

Diana: You know, you're really not all that villainous...for the devil.

Lucien replied with an emoji of a devil smiley face with horns.

Diana rolled her eyes with a laugh, lifted Seth up from the edge of her bed, and rubbed her cheek against his fur.

"Don't wait up for me."

Seth's purr was like a small car's motor, rumbling away as he moved his head so he could rub his cheeks against her chin, and then she set him back down. He flopped onto his side and twitched his tail back and forth as he watched her smooth her skirt down, and then she snatched her purse and waved at him.

When she got down to the car waiting for her, her mind was miles away. Tonight felt...special. She couldn't explain why, but she had that sense in the air that something was going to happen, something good. It made the fine hairs stand up on her neck, like the way the air seemed tense with energy before a thunderstorm, and she liked the feeling. She looked out the window as they drove their usual route. When the rain started, she smiled and traced the droplets on the window with her fingertip, watching their paths blend and blur over and over as the storm grew.

"Sure hope you guys are staying inside tonight," Douglas said as he cranked the windshield wipers higher to see through the storm.

"We're going to the opera, but I don't mind the rain." She winked at the driver through the reflection of the rearview mirror.

Diana sat back in the car and closed her eyes, trying to picture her and Lucien sitting at the opera. He would look so sexy in his black suit.

"Shit!" Douglas's curse was the last thing she remembered before the world spun out of control. She tumbled like a tiny fragment of colored glass in a giant kaleidoscope. The shriek of metal and the hiss of shattered glass surrounded her, and pain exploded through her as the car came to a rocking halt. She couldn't breathe, the air simply wouldn't fill her lungs.

"Lucien!" She screamed his name inside her head.

"Diana!" His voice was there, echoing in her head, or was it outside? She reached through the broken window, unable to move, and every bone in her body felt shattered.

"Diana!" This time she was certain Lucien was there. Somehow he'd found her, had come, but it was too late. She could feel the living part of her...dying. It was the most curious sensation. Her heart was so full of sorrow. She didn't want to leave him, didn't want to lose those sacred, secret hours between midnight and dawn with him.

I love you...I love you with everything that I am, with my last breath. She willed her thoughts out into the universe, praying he would somehow hear her. The pain that had seconds ago felt so crippling was drifting away, like a wisp of smoke from an extinguished candle.

Where goes the smoke, so shall I...to lands far and away from here. She wanted to stay with Lucien, but she knew it wouldn't be possible.

White clouds slowly built around her, cushioning her with warmth, and then she saw it, the gleaming towers and endless rays of light. Heaven was everything she'd always dreamed it would be, but Lucien wasn't there with her.

I would give anything to go back to him. Anything.

There would be no deal with the devil to bring her back. It was far too late.

🕸

TEN MINUTES EARLIER

"You're doing it again," Andras grumbled.

"Doing what?" Lucien studied his clothes in the full-length mirror. He'd chosen a dark-blue tie tonight, abandoning his red one for the first time since...well, ever.

"Humming like some lovestruck fool." Andras leaned back against the desk in Lucien's office in the penthouse apartment and crossed his arms over his chest, scowling.

"Lovestruck fool?" Lucien raised a brow, challenging Andras. "Don't make me assign you to the housewives' circle of hell."

At the stark terror on his friend's face, Lucien chuckled. It was about time the other fallen angel gave him the respect he was due.

"I'm not lovestruck. You know that isn't even possible. I'm just pleased, very pleased with how Diana is coming along. She lets me do the most... Well, let me put it this way, Andras—you'd be humming too if you had a woman like her in bed." He wasn't lying, and Andras knew it.

Lucien had spent the last few weeks with Diana, spending more than simply Friday nights together. They'd spent entire days together, dinner, dancing, movies, picnics, things he would have scorned before he met her. Now they were the things that kept him smiling, kept him feeling light-hearted even when he had to return to the dark pits of hell to do his job.

"You only have a little more time with her. It's better if you start weaning yourself off now."

"She's not an addiction," Lucien snapped as he whirled to face his friend. "She's just a bit of fun." The lie rang in the air between them, like the ringing of a bell.

"All I'm saying is that you need to focus. You still haven't recovered from the *rabishu* attacks. I'm worried about you, that's all. You can barely even jump between places these days."

"You better make yourself scarce. She'll be here soon." Lucien checked his watch. It was close to eight o'clock. He couldn't wait to show Diana what he had planned tonight. Dinner after the opera and then bed in Iceland in a special clear bubbled room that would let them make love beneath the stars for hours. He wanted to remember every single night with her, burn her into his memory so deeply that she would never leave him, even after centuries had passed.

I have to keep a part of her, always.

Lucien glanced back in the mirror and saw it, the vulnerability in his eyes. Andras was right. He had formed an attachment to Diana, one that ran far too deep to be wise, but he couldn't seem to deny himself what he wanted, which was her. Yet when the contract ended in a month, he would have to. If he didn't make a clean break, he would want to keep her, and then he would have to watch her age and die. He couldn't stand the thought. He checked his watch again and smiled. Soon she would be here, soon—

Pain knifed through him, and he fell to one knee, clutching his chest.

"Ah!" he cried out as visions dashed across his closed eyes.

Rain, heavy on the roads, the car, the slick roads. Steel groaning, tires screeching, glass shattering. Blood on the windshield.

"Diana!" Lucien knew she was in danger, and his powers were nearly gone. He rushed to the glass case that held his last feather. He smashed the glass and gripped the feather, feeling the bright flood of power, the last bit of his grace. He tucked it into his coat before he summoned the last of his powers and flashed in an instant to where Diana was.

Rain fell hard and cold on his skin as he stumbled down to the ditch where the black sedan was resting. Smoke curled up from the engine, and glass littered the slick grass.

"Diana!" He called her name again as he knelt by the overturned car. The driver was coughing and winced as he fought to get free of his seat and crawl from the vehicle.

"Mr. Star...I'm so sorry..." The man collapsed onto his back and blacked out.

But Lucien wasn't focused on him. He stared at Diana. She was lying limp on her side, blood oozing from her temple, one hand extended out the window.

Numb, Lucien reached out to touch her hand. Her fingers curled around his, like a child's, weak and tentative. He could *feel* her lifeblood slipping away. He summoned everything inside him to heal her, but...nothing came. He withdrew his feather, putting it into her hands, hoping that if she came into contact with his grace now, it would jolt her back to life. The feather glinted and shimmered beneath the rain, but Diana remained motionless.

"You can't save her, brother." The familiar voice came from behind him. He didn't need to turn to see who it was. Michael, the archangel. He hadn't faced Michael in more than a thousand years. They'd once been brothers, but since the fall, they'd been bitter enemies. Seeing Michael here, now, when the world felt like it was ending around him seemed like a private joke between them. But Michael wasn't laughing.

"Why can't I save her?" Lucien asked, his voice low and rough. His throat was tight, and he felt like he couldn't breathe. The last time he'd felt this way was when his wings had been ripped from his back, by none other than the angel standing beside him.

"Her life has had a particular purpose. Her destiny was never to be controlled by you."

"Her destiny?" The words tasted cold and alien upon Lucien's tongue as sorrow, an emotion he'd long forgotten how to feel, now wrapped around him like a death shroud.

"She has had a far greater purpose than you know. It's why Jimiel had orders to protect her."

Lucien curled his hand more tightly around Diana's fingers as a torment he'd never known he could feel began to rip him apart.

"Go away and let me mourn," he told Michael. "Have your fun another day. I will not let you destroy my last moments with her." Hot tears coursed down his cheeks, and he did not wipe them away.

I am changed. She changed me. His angelic soul was wounded and crying for relief, but what could he do? His powers could not match his father's.

"You cry for a human, Lucifer?" Michael asked, his righteous tone fading. Now he seemed only puzzled.

"She was...my *everything*." She was supposed to be the pure soul to keep hell's gates strong, but from that first night together she'd been something infinitely more precious.

She was my heaven...and I've lost paradise a second time.

"But she cannot be everything. Only our father is," Michael insisted.

Lucien shook his head. "Love...that's what makes her everything." *Love.* He'd seen her love in a hundred different ways. The way she smiled just after waking, the way she laughed when he put pineapples in the grocery basket, the way she gave her soul away to save her father, the way she said she loved him with sweet kisses long after midnight had faded into dawn and she didn't have to stay with him yet she did.

"You love her?" Michael stiffened.

It shouldn't be possible, but somehow it was. He had fallen in love with a mortal, and now he was losing her. It was like he was falling all over again, the wind whipping his face, his back bleeding with the loss of his wings, and the awful aching inside his chest. Losing love was like losing his grace. He couldn't survive that pain, not again. Grief weighed heavily upon him, and the scars on his back itched fiercely. If he still had his wings, he would've cloaked himself with them to hide his breaking heart.

"I do. I love her more than anything." He couldn't forget that moment in the hospital chapel when Diana had agreed to do anything to save her father. For love. He finally understood that truly human emotion in a way no angel ever could.

"Lucifer." Jimiel suddenly appeared, breathless, his face ashen. He glanced at Michael and then knelt by Lucien on the ground.

"It's not all lost. There's still time," Jimiel said.

"What?" Lucien grabbed Jimiel's arm.

"You aren't the only one who makes bargains. I've just come with the news..."

"Tell me," Lucien growled, daring to cling to the tiny thread of hope the guardian angel provided.

"Your life for hers," Jimiel said.

"My life?" He didn't understand. He was an immortal. He could not give away his life—

"You give yourself up to Father, let him reclaim you for the heavens. Your life, your very essence, will be given to her."

Comprehension dawned on Lucien. He would cease to exist. Returning to the light was an angel's way of dying. He could make the sacrifice for her that she had been willing to make for her father. A life for a life. A soul for a soul.

"If you do that for her, she will live a long and happy life. It's a promise from Father." Jimiel placed a hand over Lucien's.

"When did you find out *Lucien* was her purpose?" Michael suddenly demanded of Jimiel.

"When he felt her pain." Jimiel stared at Lucien.

"What do you mean, *I* was her purpose?" Lucien demanded. He could feel the last of her life leaving, like a trickle of a river drying up. There was no time left.

"I knew Diana's life was reserved for something special, but I wasn't allowed to know until now." Jimiel's smile was sorrowful. "She was born to save you. It's always been her fate. To find you and love you, even beyond death."

"That was her destiny?" He could barely speak as he squeezed her hand tight.

"Only one woman in the entire world could be brave enough to love the devil, and she was." Jimiel put a hand on Lucien's shoulder, and he shuddered at the comforting contact.

Lucien breathed deeply, the movement hurting like knives cutting into his heart over and over.

"We don't have much time," Jimiel cautioned. "It's your choice. You can save her. If you're brave enough to let go of your hate and simply allow yourself to love."

Love... He already loved her, and he simply hadn't known then. Could he say goodbye to the dark and surrender to the light? Give up everything he had, all this power, to save one human's life? He thought of every moment of his existence since the fall, the darkness, the pain, the agony of losing his joy, his grace, his home, his brothers, his father. It could all end. He could let it go and return to the light and save Diana.

"Yes," he whispered. "I'll do it." He curled both of his hands around Diana's. His throat constricted as he struggled to speak.

"Jimiel, swear to me she will have that life you promised. Every joy, every laugh, every love, every glorious moment in the sun. I need to hear *you* promise me that."

"I promise. Father promises. She will have it all."

"Good." Lucien relaxed, his body, heart, and soul strangely free now that he'd made the decision to let go of his hate. The storm clouds broke about them, and sunlight lit the wreckage of the car.

"I love you, Diana. No matter what happens, I will always love you." He spoke the words as his throat constricted with longing as he stole one more look at her. Then everything around him blazed brilliantly white.

The scars on his back exploded. The pain he'd held on to for millennia faded away. He had one glimpse of the glittering spires of heaven, and then he heard a voice inside his head.

"Lucifer, my brightest star in the morning. How I have loved you. How I still love you..."

Lucien felt his body coming apart, atom by atom, in an instant, and his last thought and only thought was of Diana. She would be safe. She would be loved by some lucky mortal man. A man who would never know the treasure she was, a gift from heaven. The end was over, and there was no pain. Only endless light.

LUCAS STARLING CURSED THE RAIN AS IT LASHED HIS windows, and he flicked the wiper blades on. This was seriously dangerous shit. All he wanted to do was get back to his nightclub, but he had to stop by and see a friend tonight.

"I should've stayed at the club." He turned down the highway, flicking his brights on to see through the gloom. Then he slammed on the brakes as a horrific sight came into view. A black sedan was rolled over in a ditch, smoke drifting up from the engine, the headlights piercing eerily ahead into the woods.

"Shit!" He parked his car and raced over, sliding in the mud. A man lay unconscious by the car. Lucas checked his pulse, and it was steady. Shit, he hoped that meant the guy was okay.

"Help…" A weak feminine voice drew him to the back of the car.

"Hold on!" Lucas reached into the shattered window, hissing as pain knifed his arms, but he found a woman and pulled her out to lie across his lap. She wore the most beautiful dark-blue dress he'd ever seen, like some 1950s starlet. Seeing her hurt was like a punch to his gut. A deep gash on her forehead was bleeding heavily. He dug into his pocket and pulled out his cell phone, dialing 911.

"Nine-one-one, what's your emergency?" the operator asked.

"There's been a wreck off Beckett Road. Two people are injured. Please send help!" He held on to the woman and brushed her hair back from her face. She gazed up at him with beautiful gray eyes. Something hit him like a freight train, and he held on to her like the world was ending around him. All he knew was that he couldn't let this woman die.

"My name is Lucas. I'm here to help. Stay with me, beautiful," he said.

She smiled dazedly. "You think I'm beautiful?"

"I think you're gorgeous." He meant it. He saw a lot of hot women in his nightclub, but they had nothing on this woman. There was something about her, something that made everything inside him go still. She filled him with peace.

"I love your eyes," she murmured and reached up to touch his cheek. Something inside him stirred, a strange sense of déjà vu, a flash, a memory of someone touching his face just like that.

"Keep talking," he said. "What else do you love about me?" he teased, hoping to keep her awake and alert. Distant sirens filled him with relief. An ambulance would be here soon.

"What happened?" She blinked, distracted.

"You've been in a wreck. But I've called for an ambulance. Help is on the way. So keep talking to me, okay?" He brushed his thumbs over her cheeks, completely absorbed by this woman. It was as though she glowed...not that he could explain it, exactly. The rain misted on her face, forming tiny diamond-like drops on the tips of her eyelashes, and he wanted to kiss her like he'd never wanted anything else in his life. Kiss her and make her whole.

"Stay with me?" she asked. "I don't want to be alone."

"You won't be, beautiful. I promise." And he meant it. Whoever this woman was, he was not about to let her go.

EPILOGUE

WHAT IN ME IS DARK, ILLUMINE. —JOHN MILTON, PARADISE LOST

Six years later

Diana touched the faint scar at her hairline. Even all these years after the accident, she still couldn't forget the night that everything had changed.

"Beautiful?" Lucas joined her at the mirror, curling his arms around her waist.

She gazed at him through the reflection. He was so gorgeous, with dark hair and soft brown eyes, and he was wicked too, her husband, a real sin in bed. From the moment they met, she'd felt like she'd known him forever, like they'd loved each other in another life. Diana knew it sounded crazy, but she couldn't deny it. She loved him, loved him so much it hurt.

"I was just thinking about the night we met." Their eyes locked before his lashes fanned down as he pressed a kiss to her cheek.

"I still dream about it," he admitted, his voice hoarse with emotion. "If I had been a moment too late…"

She turned in his arms and kissed away his worries. "You weren't too late. You were right on time to save me." She cupped his face and stood on her tiptoes to kiss him again, their lips meeting in a soft, exploring kiss. It was the strangest thing, but sometimes when she kissed him, she thought she saw... But no, that was silly. She was in love. Surely every woman saw castles in the sky and flashes of brilliant light when they were kissing the man they loved.

"Where were you going that night? I never asked," Lucas said as he rubbed his palms up and down her back.

"You know, I can't even remember. I just had to be somewhere by midnight..." It was the one thing she couldn't forget. The need to be somewhere with someone, yet it just didn't matter now. That night was merely a bad memory, but it had led to something amazing.

"You need to come see this." Lucas tugged on her hand, and they walked to the back door and looked out at the yard.

"Amara, what are you doing?" Diana asked as she saw their four-year-old daughter clutching something in her hands. It was a long white feather that seemed to glitter as though covered with diamond dust. It was the feather that Lucas had found beside her body the night of the crash. She'd never understood how it had gotten there, or what had happened to the bird in the storm for it to leave it there, but she'd wanted to keep it. From the moment her daughter was big enough to reach for things on the shelves, she'd carried the feather around like a favorite stuffed animal.

"Mommy!" Amara clapped her hands, her blonde curls bouncing in the sun. The light created a halo on the child's head as she waved the feather. She was much like her godmother, Amara, one of Diana's friends who owned a rather curious bookshop. They'd met one day when Diana's car broke down outside Amara's store. Amara had kept her company while she'd waited for the tow truck, and they'd formed a fast friendship. It had been only a few days before Lucas had saved her life.

"She's such a little angel," Lucas said with a chuckle.

"She is indeed." Diana leaned back against his chest, and they both laughed as the wind tried to steal the feather from the child's hands, but Amara kept a tight grip on her treasured toy.

"Amara, come inside for dinner. Grandpa and Grandma will be here soon." Diana couldn't wait to tell her father the news that her architecture firm was going to be expanding to bigger offices in downtown Chicago to meet the needs of her growing client base. Her new office was close to Lucas's nightclub, which meant she'd be able to stop and have dinner with him during the week...and most likely they'd end up naked and panting on his desk or the nearest flat surface. Her husband had a healthy appetite for sex, and he fulfilled every wicked fantasy she ever had.

"What are you thinking about, love?" Lucas asked. He brushed the backs of his fingers along her cheek, and she leaned into him, relishing the warmth of his body against hers.

"About us, about how lucky I am to have you in my life." She nuzzled his throat before she tucked her head under his chin. Lucas curled his arms around her tighter, as though he was afraid she'd vanish. She'd seen it so often in his eyes, a shadow of fear that this beautiful, perfect life they shared would disappear. But she had faith it wouldn't. They could face anything together. Diana had everything she could ever want—a wonderful life, a wonderful family, and a man who had brought her back from death itself. Sometimes, deep in the night, she would wake and reach for him, needing to feel his body pressed against hers as the clock struck midnight. And he was always there. Then she knew all was well.

"I swear, my life didn't start until I met you." He tilted her head up and gently kissed her lips, but the kiss turned hotter, his tongue slipping between her lips until she was melting against him and forgetting about everything else.

Glittering spires...endless light...love unending.

"I love you," she whispered.

He nuzzled her neck. "I love you...through death and beyond."

The vow burned into her heart, like a promise of the ages, and she knew that he meant it. She couldn't imagine a world without this man in it. Someone had been looking out for her all those years ago. Sometimes she swore she must have been saved by an angel.

༻❀༺

Jimiel lingered invisible in the infinite space between beams of light as he watched Diana and her husband kiss in the doorway while their child played with a feather. What a strange and wondrous thing destiny was. The night Lucien gave his life for Diana's, the world had shifted. All traces of Lucifer had vanished from the minds of the mortals who'd met him. Andras had taken his place as the king of hell. And a human had saved Diana that night, pulling her from the car. A human man who would live a long, full life by Diana's side, just as Jimiel had promised. Humans said Father worked in mysterious ways, but there was nothing mysterious about acting out of love. Love was the one thing in the world that made sense. And Father had always loved his favorite angel, loved him so much he gave him a second chance to live.

"Have a good life, brother. Shine bright, always." Jimiel smiled at Lucas.

Lucas would never know, never remember who he'd once been, but that was good. As the brightest morning star, he deserved only the light, not the dark. Midnight always gave way to dawn, even for the devil.

ABOUT THE AUTHOR

Emma Castle has always loved reading but didn't know she loved romance until she was enduring the trials of law school. She discovered the dark and sexy world of romance novels and since then has never looked back! She loves writing about sexy, alpha male heroes who know just how to seduce women even if they are a bit naughty about it. When Emma's not writing, she may be obsessing over her favorite show Supernatural where she's a total Team Dean Winchester kind of girl!

If you wish to be added to Emma's new release newsletter eel free to contact Emma using the Sign up link on her website at www.emmacastlebooks.com or email her at emma@emmacastlebooks.com!

f facebook.com/Emmacastlebooks

twitter.com/emmacastlebooks

instagram.com/Emmacastlebooks

BB bookbub.com/authors/emma-castle

Made in United States
North Haven, CT
06 November 2023

43681864R00136